"We're alone again. They moved their search elsewhere."

"It's gone? We're safe?"

He nodded before resting his chin at the crown of her hair. He took in a deep lungful of air to steady his breathing and regain his senses. Her arms retreated to his waist and he felt her fingers press into the small of his back.

"Are you all right now?" she whispered against his collar.

"I haven't been this right since... I don't think anything's ever felt this right," he admitted, then tightened his arms around her, backpack and all, and buried his nose in the intoxicating scent of her hair.

A STRANGER ON HER DOORSTEP

USA TODAY Bestselling Author

JULIE MILLER

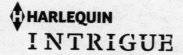

HARLEQUIN
INTRIGUE

For my hubby and fellow author, Scott E. Miller.

Thanks for helping me brainstorm this one, hon. I knew I could count on you to know your high fantasy info.

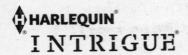

Recycling programs for this product may not exist in your area.

ISBN-13: 978-1-335-55523-6

A Stranger on Her Doorstep

Copyright © 2021 by Julie Miller

This edition published by arrangement with Harlequin Books S.A.

For questions and comments about the quality of this book, please contact us at CustomerService@Harlequin.com.

Harlequin Enterprises ULC
22 Adelaide St. West, 40th Floor
Toronto, Ontario M5H 4E3, Canada
www.Harlequin.com

Printed in U.S.A.

Julie Miller is an award-winning *USA TODAY* bestselling author of breathtaking romantic suspense—with a National Readers' Choice Award and a Daphne du Maurier Award, among other prizes. She has also earned an *RT Book Reviews* Career Achievement Award. For a complete list of her books, monthly newsletter and more, go to juliemiller.org.

Books by Julie Miller

Harlequin Intrigue

The Taylor Clan: Firehouse 13

Crime Scene Cover-Up
Dead Man District

The Precinct

Beauty and the Badge
Takedown
KCPD Protector
Crossfire Christmas
Military Grade Mistletoe
Kansas City Cop

Rescued by the Marine
Do-or-Die Bridesmaid
Personal Protection
Target on Her Back
K-9 Protector
A Stranger on Her Doorstep

Visit the Author Profile page at Harlequin.com.

CAST OF CHARACTERS

Luke Broughton/Larkin Bonecrusher—The USMC tattoo on his shoulder and a key chain with the initials L.B. are the only things that identify him. But he does know that the woman who dubs him Larkin Bonecrusher writes his favorite books. There's a light behind her scarred beauty that shines into his soul. And he's brought the danger pursuing him right to her front door.

Ava Wallace—As author A. L. Baines, she writes a bestselling series of fantasy novels. But the people of Pole Axe, Wyoming, know Ava as the damaged woman who keeps to herself. When the living, breathing embodiment of her fictional warrior hero stumbles into her life, she finally meets someone who doesn't see her as a victim.

Maxie—The Great Pyrenees is both protector and therapy dog for Ava, helping her with her PTSD.

Kent Russell—The doctor has secrets of his own.

Brandon Stout—The town sheriff was a childhood friend of Ava's.

Sue Schulman, Kris DeKamp and James Middleton—They run businesses in downtown Pole Axe.

Chapter One

Sabotage.

Luke Broughton pumped his brakes as the center line on the asphalt was gobbled up beneath the wheels of his SUV, in case it was the sharp curves and steep inclines of this mountainous highway that had caused his brakes to fail. But he knew better. He knew it in his bones.

Somebody wanted him dead.

A clearing in the trees to his left gave him a glimpse of the two black SUVs on the road above him. They were in hot pursuit, maybe a half mile behind his location. Another hairpin curve and they'd be on his tail. Until then, it was only a matter of time before his unchecked speed sent him flying off the edge of the road at the next turn he couldn't make.

He'd raced LAVs on the sand-swept roads in the Middle East and over the sparse terrain of the Afghan mountains. But this was no Light Armored Vehicle, and the Teton mountains in northwestern Wyoming were a different sort of beast. Higher, steeper elevations. Better roads but sight lines blocked by towering pines and aspen in the full leaf of summer. His knuckles whitened as he gripped the steering wheel and careened around the next curve, his rear tires fishtailing onto the shoulder before he regained control. Beyond the guardrail, there was a steep drop to the next cutback on the road. Or maybe it fell off into a rocky creek bed. Or an endless chasm filled with trees and granite outcroppings.

He tried downshifting, but his transmission had locked up on him. Definitely sabotage. Done by somebody who knew their business around ways to *accidentally* silence anyone who got in their way.

Luke laid on his horn when he saw the turkey vulture feasting on the carrion at the side of the road. The large black bird spread its enormous wings and reluctantly hopped back and floated out of harm's way as Luke plowed through the carcass. That was going to be him in about sixty seconds if he couldn't come up with a way to slow down the out-of-control SUV.

He cursed his own damn luck before risking taking one hand off the wheel to tap the front pocket of his jeans. The mini thumb drive was still there. Thank goodness he'd made himself a copy. Everything else he'd done since yesterday morning had been one rookie mistake after another. He'd been thinking like the civilian he'd been for a mere eight months, not the seasoned warrior who'd survived tours of duty overseas and fought his way through tangles of bureaucratic red tape when he'd been stationed stateside, putting together security units for the Marine Corps. Whistleblowing was a dangerous business. He should have known the illegal dealings he'd uncovered went deeper than his initial suspect.

That next turn was coming up fast. He checked his rearview mirror. The two SUVs were on the straightaway with him now, bearing down on his position. He knew what was coming—what he'd do himself if their positions were reversed and he'd been given the assignment to stop the escaping enemy by whatever means necessary.

The irony of it all was he'd been hired by Bell Design Systems to be the man driving one of those black SUVs. He hadn't realized he was the odd man out—that the enemy was someone he'd trusted, one of the men or women on his team, someone who should have had his back instead of chasing down his runaway vehicle on a remote mountain road with the express purpose of taking him out.

He steered around the next curve, careening into the guardrail and peeling the paint off the passenger side of his SUV as metal screeched against metal. He wondered if the guardrail was secure enough to stop his momentum, or if he'd have better luck turning the car into the ditch and rock face on his left. Risk sailing into the unknown or smash into solid granite? He didn't like his options. Even if he survived a purposeful crash, he'd have to pray he didn't flip the vehicle, and that he could get out fast enough to take out the other men or lose them in this vast, verdant wilderness he wasn't all that familiar with. Although he wore a gun strapped to his belt and another in an ankle holster, he had no idea how many men were in those vehicles besides the drivers. He could shoot. He could fight hand-to-hand. But one man against a potential army was never good odds.

He swerved into the oncoming lane, overcorrecting the curve, and glanced ahead at the road signs indicating a trio of tiny towns and a descent that was only going to get steeper.

"Think, Broughton." *How do I survive this?*

He should have checked the SUV before starting the engine and leaving the Ridgerunner Lodge, the fancy executive resort retreat owned by BDS on the southern end of Jackson Hole between the Snake River and Bridger-Teton National Forest. Less than a year out of the Corps and he was getting soft. Why had he agreed to meet the security chief, CEO and other company muckety-mucks in the remote location instead of corporate headquarters in Cheyenne?

And neither of those had been his first mistake. He'd handed over the evidence he'd uncovered to a source he hadn't checked and checked again. This wasn't the Corps. In the Marines, he'd trusted his senior officers without question. But he was a civilian now. His supervisor? The company bosses? His coworkers at Bell Design Systems? He hadn't personally vetted them. They hadn't gone through the same training he had at Quantico or Lejeune. They hadn't shared the same deployments or worked with a smooth-running team at Camp Arifjan or Fort Leonard Wood. The chain of command was clearly a lot sketchier in the civilian world, and he'd exposed his position like a damned private who hadn't seen battle yet.

He swore again as the speedometer crept past the eighty-mile-per-hour mark. More than thirty miles above the recommended speed limit.

The SUVs behind him were picking up speed, too. Tinted windows and the need to control his own runaway vehicle kept him from identifying his pursuers.

He suspected he'd stumbled onto something big when he'd run his security check on the executives visiting from China. He was too good at his job. Too thorough to ignore the red flags of classified communications that indicated someone within the company had a private agenda for meeting with their guests this weekend. Although he hadn't been able to pinpoint the source of the communications, the cryptic emails had been clear enough. This meeting was more than a scenic tour of Yellowstone and Teton National Park, with a couple of days set aside to lay the groundwork for a legal trade agreement. Someone intended to *illegally* sell BDS weapons technology to the Chinese. Maybe not the Chinese government. But there were enterprising souls on both sides who intended to turn a tidy profit at the expense of military and civilian lives right here in the US and among its allies. Technology meant to improve the side Captain Luke Broughton, USMC Retired, had fought for going on fifteen years before the old injury to his right leg and one concussion too many had forced him into early retirement. They'd offered him a desk job until he made lieutenant colonel, but he couldn't see staring at four walls and paperwork for another four years. He'd been raised in the Missouri Ozarks. Hunting, fishing, hiking, camping, anything outdoors, had always been his calling until a savvy recruiter had sold him on four years of college and a career serving his country.

Taking the job on the security team at Bell Design Systems had ticked all the right civilian boxes. He couldn't beat the Wyoming-based company for a location this close to the mountains and all the outdoor activities he loved. And, in a way, he'd felt like he was still serving his country, working for a firm that developed technology used primarily by the military and law enforcement. He wasn't the brains of designing the tech. But his recent military experience made him an experienced consultant, and his background with base and advanced guard security gave him the perfect skill set for being part of the multibillion-dollar company's security team.

Luke sailed around the next curve and felt his inward tires leave the road.

"Options, Broughton," he ground through clenched teeth. He needed options.

He was screwed unless he found an exit ramp or gravel road that would take him back up the mountain at an easier slope, slowing his speed enough to jump from the vehicle.

He felt the first tap to his bumper. The SUV skidded from lane to lane, but Luke fought to maintain control.

Oh, yeah. These bastards wanted him dead.

He'd survived explosions, a knife fight and a shattered leg. But you blow one whistle on someone who's supposed to be one of the good guys and there was hell to pay.

Maybe this was how he was going out.

But damned if the enemy got to win.

He had the backup evidence in his pocket. Even if he was dead on the side of the road, those maniacs would pat him down and take whatever they wanted so that not even the undertaker could trace their illegal activities. Or maybe they'd plant something on his body. Make him the scapegoat in case their scheme became public knowledge.

He needed to protect himself. He needed to get the information through to an outside ally who could help. He needed to complete this mission.

Luke pushed his gun aside and dipped his fingers into his pocket to pull out the thumb drive. This was going to hurt like a son of a gun going down, but it was the only way to secure the evidence. He jammed the data stick into his mouth and swallowed.

When the first black SUV tapped his bumper again, Luke only had one hand on the wheel.

And that was all she wrote. There was no recovering from the skid this time. He slapped both hands on the wheel, but it was too late.

The SUV tilted onto two wheels, hit the guardrail and bounced back across the road. He steered into the skid but sped off the shoulder into the ditch. A tree ripped off the side mirror and the front fender glanced off the rock wall, flipping the vehicle back onto the road.

Luke smacked his head against the window despite the airbag deploying. The seat belt locked up across his chest, stealing the air from his lungs. The crunching sound of metal was deafening. Sparks on burning asphalt stung his nose. His vision blurred as the SUV tumbled and tumbled. He blacked out for a few seconds before the SUV rocked to a halt.

He was nauseous, disoriented when he came to. Sharp, bruising pain made it difficult to catch his breath and his head felt like a spongy mess. Two men dragged him away from the wreckage.

But he was sentient enough to know that this was no rescue.

The men dropped him with a thud on the side of the road between the twisted bulk of his SUV and the mangled guardrail. He tried to raise his eyelids and peer through his lashes, but he couldn't focus. He was on his back, looking up at a platoon of men gathering around him.

Faceless men in suits and ties. Even in his groggy state, he knew that wasn't how the enemy dressed. Had he been taken hostage? Had he been tortured and lost consciousness? Had his LAV hit a roadside bomb? Where was the rest of his team?

There were hands on him, and he was being searched. They removed his phone. He nearly retched when they rolled him and took his wallet. He felt a pinch at the back of his neck and knew they had ripped off his dog tags.

His eyelids were too heavy to keep open now. But he was still conscious enough to mentally assess his injuries. Another concussion. The coppery taste of blood at the corner of his mouth. Something stabbing him inside.

Radio for backup. Extraction! Extraction!

He had a vague notion that help wasn't coming. The enemy had him at their mercy. But the color of the world he'd glimpsed through his lashes was too green for Afghanistan or Iraq. The Hurt Locker never had a cool breeze like the one whispering across his face.

Suicide bomber must have made it past a check-point. Snider! Martinez! Sound off! Where were the rest of his men?

"It's not on him," he heard a voice say. "Maybe he didn't make a copy."

"He's too smart not to." That sounded like the man in charge. "I don't want anyone to link the body to us. Grab his gun, too. If the authorities ever find him, they'll be able to track him by the serial number."

"What about his car?"

"I'll take care of it." A third voice. Who were these men? Soldiers? Guards?

"It's a company loaner. Take it apart in case he stashed it there. We'll erase his name from the records."

That wasn't military talk. This wasn't right. He wasn't in the Corps anymore.

But damned if he could force any of this to make sense.

Gravel crunched the pavement beside his ear as someone stood over him, casting a shadow over his face. "I could have used a man like you. Too bad you couldn't see my point of view. I could have made you very rich." The shadow left and sunlight washed over his face again. "Put a bullet in his head and make this all go away."

Shake it off. Clear your head. How are you going to survive when the enemy captures you?

He heard multiple footsteps and a car engine

turning over. He heard someone calling for a tow truck. They didn't do that out in the field.

Where was he?

What was happening?

Who were these men?

How did he get hurt?

How are you going to survive?

His CO's advice echoed in his head. He'd been trained to fight. To give the enemy grief. To do whatever it took to stay alive and complete his mission.

Forcing his leaden eyelids open to a swirling blur of blue sky and green treetops, of twisted metal and rocky outcroppings and pinpricks of light that pierced his brain, he took in his surroundings. Car wreck. A sliver of understanding warred with the pinpricks of light for control of his brain.

Shadows of men walked to another vehicle. There was nothing to his left beyond the grassy edge and some wildflowers beneath the shredded guardrail that had done its job to save him from certain death. He could feel the bulk of metal in his boot. A gun. If he could reach it... The world spun into oblivion when he tried to move. He quickly squeezed his eyes shut and breathed deeply, willing himself to stay conscious. Staying awake was the only way he could fight.

Put a bullet in his head and make this all go away.

He needed options. Now.

Option A. Was there any way he could reach his gun and stand his ground here on the road? Hell, he wasn't even sure he could stand.

Option B. What lay in the abyss below his line of sight? Was he physically able to make a run for it? Was escape a possibility?

A shadow fell over him again. He heard the unmistakable sound of a bullet being loaded into a chamber.

"You're awake?" His would-be killer hesitated. Yeah. It was a hell of a thing to look a man in the eye when you pulled the trigger.

The man squatted beside him and pressed two thick fingers to his neck. Then he muttered a curse at determining he hadn't cooperated by dying for him. "Nothing personal, Captain. Orders are orders."

The man pushed to his feet and took aim.

Option B.

Luke rolled. He bet every heartbeat left in him that he wasn't plunging to his death as he slipped beneath the guardrail and tumbled off the overhang into the abyss.

The man with the gun swore.

He heard the crack of a gunshot, felt a burning hot poker drill through his shoulder. And then he was falling.

He dropped a good ten feet until he crashed into the first ledge. But loose gravel and his momentum carried him over the edge, and he hit another rocky outcropping, jarring a fresh wave of pain through his side. He instinctively snatched at a sapling growing out of a fissure between the rocks, then tall grass, flowers, rocks, anything he could claw his grip into.

He heard more bullets.

The answering whiff of air and sharp pings of the tiny missiles hitting a rock or tree or dirt created a cacophonous symphony that chased his crazy fall down the mountain.

By the time he slammed to a stop near a copse of trees at the bottom of the ravine, his battered body and jumbled brain made him think he should be dead.

He prayed the man with the gun on the road above him thought the same.

HE'D BEEN RUNNING for hours.

Well, *running* was a relative term, considering how often he'd stumbled or fallen. But he'd kept moving. He hoped to hell it hadn't been in circles. It was hard to get his bearings with all these trees and no compass. Yet even with throbbing gelatin for a brain, he knew enough to keep going downhill. Away from the bullets. Away from the option of winding up dead. He'd followed the current of the creek, had even walked through the icy, rushing water itself for half a mile or so to avoid leaving footsteps and any scent that could be tracked, in case whoever was after him had dogs.

At least the cold water had stimulated his senses and kept him conscious when every weary bone in his body begged him to lie down and sleep. He'd torn up the button-down shirt he'd been wearing to tie off a bandage for the hole in his shoulder. He'd stemmed the bleeding for a little while, but now his shirt was soaked and the blood was trickling down his arm again, leaving a distinct trail of red droplets for anyone who had the skills to track him through the trees, scrubby grass and exposed gray rock of the mountain. He hoped he hadn't attracted the attention of some bear or mountain lion—they'd be able to follow the blood trail, too.

He'd sustained an injury to his head. Although his hair was cropped close to his scalp, it was matted with blood. But without a mirror or proper med kit, he had no way of assessing or treating the wound.

He could feel cognition slipping away as steadily as his life's blood was ebbing from his body. Only his training was keeping him alive.

Imminent threat. Behind enemy lines. Keep moving.

Why was he running? How did he get hurt? Was he being followed?

He'd never heard any footsteps or vehicle pursuing him. Only a serious climber or someone willing to break his neck and fall like he had could make that descent quickly. He'd avoided anything that resembled a road or even a hiking path, so trailing him in a vehicle was next to impossible. Why did he think he was being chased? Someone tried to kill him. Someone nearly succeeded.

Who was the enemy?

Keep moving.

He caught the toe of his boot on a rock and stumbled. He paid dearly for the instinct to catch himself. Pain ripped through his wounded shoulder and bum knee, and his lungs seized up in his chest.

Medic. He needed to reach a medic.

If he didn't get help, he would be dead soon. He rolled onto his back and gazed up at the dark green of pine needles and the lighter green of deciduous leaves arching high over his head. Trees like that didn't grow in the sand. And he was wearing jeans, not a uniform. He mentally shook off his confused thoughts. "You're stateside, Captain. You're out of the Corps."

Captain. The Corps. That meant he was a Marine.

That didn't mean he knew where he was in the good ol' US of A.

He had a feeling there was a lot he didn't know.

He squeezed his eyes shut against the dapples of light dancing through the trees. Every now and then, the lights hit his retinas straight-on, piercing his brain like shrapnel. He'd taken a hard blow to the head. He fought the urge to surrender to his fatigue or succumb to the dizziness that made him want to puke.

So he dragged himself to his feet and kept moving.

Find help. Survive.

He felt the ground change beneath his feet before he recognized the clearing in the trees. The grass, dirt and pine needles gave way to the crunch of tiny rocks beneath his boots. The uneven terrain became a relatively flat surface. A gravel road. No, a driveway.

Driveways led to houses or businesses.

Driveways led to help.

The gravel was evenly distributed and there were no ruts in the road, making him think it hadn't been used very often. He'd made a pretty fair assessment of how isolated this place was long before he crested a rise and saw the two-story log cabin with an attached garage and a heavy-duty pickup truck parked out front.

The porch ran the width of the house, and there were big pots of colorful flowers on either side of the steps he tripped up. He heard a dog's loud, deep barking before he ever reached the front door and knocked.

Maybe he should rethink this. Guard dog? Sounded like a big one with that booming voice. Unknown location? What if he'd circled back to the very doorstep he'd been running from?

He swiped his palm across the bristly buzz cut of hair on his head and came away with blood on his fingers, making the desperate decision for him. He braced that bloody hand against the doorjamb, falling weakly against it before pounding the door with his fist again.

The dog's bark vibrated the door beneath his hand. It definitely didn't sound friendly. But the grain of the wood beneath his hand was spinning into bizarre patterns, and he wasn't sure if it was his eyes or his thoughts that couldn't keep things straight anymore.

He heard a chain scrape across the inside of the door. A dead bolt flipped open. There was a sharp, sotto voce command and the dog fell silent a split second before the door swung open.

"Sorry to bother you, but…"

He stared into the twin barrels of an over-under shotgun.

The dog was a big, white furry thing with black markings around its eyes and muzzle. But the dog wasn't what captured his attention. He was caught by a pair of blue eyes, dark like cobalt and twilight skies and every hushed, intriguing fantasy he'd ever had about a woman.

"I don't like surprise visitors. What do you want?" She was a little younger than him, probably in her thirties, but there was no mistaking that she had the advantage here.

"I'm wounded. Need help. Can you call an ambulance?"

"Is this some kind of joke? Who are you?"

"My blood and your shotgun are a joke?" Who had a sick sense of humor like that?

"How do I know that blood is real?"

He had no answer for that.

She shook her head slowly from side to side, stirring the long cascade of coffee-colored hair that hung in a loose ponytail over one shoulder and revealing the long, thin scar that curved from her cheek to her jaw. If the gun wasn't evidence enough, he could see that this woman was a warrior. "You run along. I don't sign books for desperate fans who trespass on my property. And I won't reward your cleverness or diligence in tracking me down by writing you into one of my stories."

Her words made no sense. He must have taken a really hard blow to the head. "What are you talking about?"

"Call 9-1-1 yourself. Don't bother me again."

He was leaning heavily on his good shoulder now, the sturdiness of the house about the only thing holding him up. "No phone," he managed to eke out. "Please. I need...sanctuary. Place to rest...to think..."

She shook her head, but the gun never wavered. "The last time a stranger asked for my help..."

He saw the muscle of uncertainty twitching in her jaw, the fear and compassion warring in her expression. Yet he knew the moment her eyes hardened like dark ice that she'd made the decision not to help him.

He pushed away from the door, willed his legs to hold him upright, even though that made him a good six inches taller than her and probably looked like he was trying to threaten her. "I fell down the mountain, lady. I've been shot," he argued. There was more to tell her, but he couldn't find the words. "I swear I won't hurt you."

"I've heard that before, too." That's when he saw the other scars. Through the spinning haze of his vision, he spotted the matching puckers of healed skin on each hand. There was another at the vee of her tank top beneath the long-sleeved blouse she wore. He recognized marks like that. She'd been tortured. Some time ago, because every mark had healed, and he glimpsed the patch of what had been a skin graft along the underside of her arm, beneath the cuff of her rolled-up sleeve.

Fists of anger and compassion squeezed around his heart at the suffering she had endured. "Whatever happened to you, I won't—"

"Town's that way." She inclined her head to the left. "They've got a clinic." With the shotgun still aimed at him, she tossed that beautiful ponytail behind her back and retreated a step. "Maxie, heel."

The dog retreated with her and she closed the door in his face.

The decisive click of the dead bolt and the scrape of the chain locking him out sent the clear message that he wasn't finding refuge here.

When he didn't immediately leave, she shouted through the door. "I'll call the sheriff if you don't go."

Yes. Do that. The sheriff can help me. He needed to say the words, but his body was shutting down. His brain was refusing to work.

If he were one hundred percent, he could bust down the door and overpower the woman. But he was closer to ten percent, probably less than that, and the pellets from that shotgun would be embedded in his chest before he could even break through a window, much less get to her phone.

He turned, looking for the next option, but the forested mountainside swirled into a miasma of greens and grays. His knees buckled and the world faded away as he collapsed onto the porch.

Chapter Two

Ava cringed at the thud from the other side of the locked door. "Don't do that. Do not need my help."

She peeked through the window beside the door and saw dusty, grass-stained jeans and a broad back sprawled across the edge of her porch and top step. He looked different from this angle, unexpectedly vulnerable and deceptively harmless without the stern line of his bearded jaw and piercing silvery-green eyes. A bloodstained wad of material had fallen loose from beneath the shoulder seam of his missing sleeve. Trickles of blood mingled with lines and curves of an intricate tattoo adorning his upper arm and circling the firm muscles of his biceps and triceps. More blood seeped from a gash and goose egg above his left ear, soaking into the collar of his blue shirt. With trembling hands, Ava hugged the shotgun to her chest and pressed her back against the door, turning away from the man on her doorstep. "Oh, damn. He's really hurt."

Or was this a really convincing charade?

She'd fallen for that once before. And it had nearly cost her everything.

A blow to the head. Waking up blindfolded and cold. Strapped to a wooden chair that left splinters in her back and thighs because she was wearing nothing more than her bra and panties. But that discomfort was only the beginning of her pain.

Just as panicked thoughts clouded her vision, she felt a soft bump against her hip and a cold nose nuzzling her hand where she held the shotgun. Ava blinked away the traumatic memories that threatened to overwhelm her and looked down into the big white dog's steady black eyes. Ava dropped her hand from the butt of her shotgun to smooth her palm across Maxie's warm head and bury her fingers in the dog's thick white-and-black coat.

"Good girl, Maxie." Although she'd gotten the Great Pyrenees as a guard dog to give her advance warning of anyone coming within shouting distance of her isolated cabin, the gentle giant had turned out to be a natural therapy dog. More than keeping Ava company while she avoided the world that had nearly killed her, Maximillia Madrona Draconella Reine—named after the lead dragon character in the books she wrote, and answering to the more practical Maxie—had sensed, even as a puppy, when Ava's post-traumatic stress was kicking in and the waking nightmares were filling her head. The big, furry caretaker had learned to touch Ava, even crawl into bed and lie down beside her if necessary, to offer strength and comfort—a warm body to cling to and dark eyes or a gentle touch to focus on whenever the panic attacks threatened, or the flashbacks dragged her into the terrors from her past. With Maxie at her side, Ava had learned to handle the simple intricacies of human interaction again—when it was on her terms and in small, planned doses.

Surprise visits from dangerous-looking men who were bleeding on her front porch hadn't been checked off her list of encounters she was comfortable with yet. After the weekend two years earlier that had changed her face, her life and her ability to trust, she might never be comfortable with things she couldn't control.

Weekly check-ins with her online therapist assured her she was improving, that she was more than capable of returning to *normal*, given enough time. Dr. Foster had promised Ava that trusting her own instincts was the first step to learning to trust others again. She trusted Maxie. She trusted her therapist. She trusted her editor and agent in New York, so long as she didn't have to travel there to see them in person. She trusted that leaving Chicago and moving to her late grandparents' isolated cabin in the mountains near Pole Axe, Wyoming, where she'd spent the summers of her childhood was the right decision for her. Here she could find the space and healing surroundings she needed. She'd found comfort and security in the dog by her side. She'd found confidence in the weapons training and self-defense courses she'd taken. And with every cautious foray into town, she'd reconnected with old friends and was on her way to making new ones. Given enough time, she'd learn to interact with the real world as easily as she did the fictional world of fantasy creatures and noble quests that she wrote about. She hoped.

Ava concentrated on the soft texture of Maxie's fur beneath her fingers and inhaled deeply. She could do this. Here in Wyoming she was the anonymous Ava Wallace, big-city transplant turned small-town girl who'd inherited her grandparents' cabin. Despite her quiet, cautious life, she was accepted in Pole Axe because she was Jim and Myrna Wallace's granddaughter, not because she was A. L. Baines, the *New York Times* bestselling author who'd disappeared from the limelight at the peak of her success. Here, she wasn't the obsession of a depraved kidnapper. She could answer her front door to help a neighbor, or even a tall, desperate stranger with silvery-green eyes and intertwining tattoos she was far too curious to identify.

Every survival instinct that made her a well-armed recluse, who lived as far off the grid as her necessary links to technology allowed, warred with her innate compassion. She knew better than most what it was like to be desperately hurt and at the mercy of another. The old Ava wouldn't have hesitated. But caring had gotten her into trouble before. Compassion had nearly gotten her killed.

She rubbed her cheek against the gun's cool steel barrel before clutching it in a firm grip once more. "Damn it, Maxie, we have to help him."

A soft, deep woof backed up her resolute vow to help the man outside.

"This better not be a trick." Ava unhooked the chain and dead bolt and opened the door, urging Maxie out ahead of her. Tucking the butt of the gun against her shoulder, she kept it aimed at the intruder's back as she crossed the wood planks of the porch. Although she wielded a gun instead of a bow and arrow, she could put on a tough-chick facade like Willow Storm, the heroine in her books. Ava nudged her toe against the man's boot, as far away from the blood and potentially grabbing hands as she could get. "Hey, mister? Are you dead?"

Right. Because he'd answer that question with a yes if he was. With no reply to either her voice or her boot, Ava exhaled a resolute breath and propped the shotgun just inside the door, beyond the man's reach if he came to. Maxie sat with curious eyes near the man's head, panting, as Ava knelt beside him and checked for hidden weapons and identification, a hard-earned skill she wished she'd known two years earlier.

Starting at his leather boots, she dipped her fingers inside. No hidden knife. She found an ankle holster with a short-nosed Springfield Armory pistol, which she removed. After discovering it was loaded, but that there was no bullet in the chamber, she tucked the weapon into the back of her jeans. Unless she squeezed the trigger, she knew the safety was engaged. Teaching literature and composition at a small college in Chicago, and attending Renaissance fairs and Comicons to get ideas to make up spells and to portray her fictional costumes and weaponry with accuracy in her books, she never would have expected that she'd become an expert in modern guns, knives and homemade torture devices. Her reaction to the stranger's weapon was clinical—identify its potential threat, neutralize it, move on to the next task. Allowing herself the luxury of feeling shock or fear would only delay her reaction in ensuring her own safety. That sort of discipline had been a hard lesson to learn. Now those routine assessments were second nature to her. It was the only way she could get through personal encounters anymore.

But there was something about running her hands along the man's warm, muscular calves and thighs, then cupping the back pockets of his jeans to find he carried no wallet with identification on him, which spoke to something purely female and purposefully forgotten deep inside her. Lord, she hadn't touched a man with anything other than a handshake since… She squeezed her eyes shut as a phantom pain sliced across her cheek. "Damn it, Ava. Stay in the moment."

Maxie moved to sit beside her, leaning against her and nearly toppling her over. Ava laughed before the tears could take hold and hugged her arms around her furry caretaker's neck. "I'll be okay, girl. Come on. Let's turn this guy over."

Not that she needed the help, but it reminded Ava she wasn't truly alone when the big dog propped a paw on the man's uninjured arm and seemed to pull him with Ava off the top step until he lay flat on his back on the porch. Then her curious dog lowered her head and sniffed the stranger, nuzzling his neck with her cold, wet nose before slurping her tongue across his abraded jawline. "Maxie!" she chided, nudging the dog back to a more sanitary distance.

But the raspy stroke of the dog's tongue roused the man a little. A deep-pitched moan vibrated in his throat and he repeated the last word he'd heard in a husky whisper. "Maxie..."

"Mister? Can you tell me your name?" It was then that she realized that her truck was the only vehicle parked in the driveway. Maxie hadn't alerted to a car driving up. The dog had heard his footsteps on the gravel and jumped up, barking an alarm while Ava pulled her shotgun from the gun safe. "How did you get here? How did you get hurt?"

It wasn't hard to assess his injuries from this angle. Blood in a beard that was longer than the hair on his head. Scrapes and bruises along almost every sharp angle of his face and body—knuckles, elbows, knees. He'd taken a bad fall—or several of them. The hole in his shoulder was from a bullet. She picked up the wad of sleeve material he'd torn from his shirt and gently wiped the blood from his arm, giving her a clearer look at the tattoo he bore. An eagle sitting atop a globe with an anchor behind it. The words *Semper Fi* and numbers she assumed were a significant date circled the hollow of sinewed skin beneath the jut of his shoulder muscle. Muscles. Lots of muscles. He was big and built like a prizefighter…or a medieval swordsman. This man had been trained for battle. Despite her own self-defense instruction, if this guy were more cognizant, he'd easily be able to overpower her.

Just imagining the possibility of their positions being reversed, with her at his mercy and him armed and towering over her, sent a chill rippling down her spine. She rocked back onto her heels, needing to put some distance between them and get her head right again. "Come on, Ava. You've got Willow Storm's spirit running through your veins. You can handle this."

"Willow Storm—" he echoed, never opening his eyes "—can handle anything."

"What?" He wasn't exactly parroting her words this time, but he wasn't making sense, either. Ava squeezed the man's chin, carefully avoiding the scrape there, and turned his undeniably masculine face to hers. "Are you awake or not? Sergeant? Lieutenant?"

Mr. Dying on Her Front Doorstep.

She couldn't let that happen.

"Need medic...call team for extraction..."

"Extraction?" Oh, wow, was this guy out of it. "You have a team around here?" Of course not. Even if he were part of a National Guard unit starting their weekend drill, they wouldn't be on maneuvers in blue jeans and dress shirts. Would they? And though neatly trimmed, that beard would be the first thing to go, right? This man was alone, and he was in trouble. She'd been too suspicious to believe his plea for help. Now she hoped she hadn't waited too long to act.

Ava tossed the soiled cloth to the ground and uncurled her legs to dash inside the cabin to retrieve clean towels and a first-aid kit. When she returned and knelt beside him again, she could see that the wound had reopened without the cotton material he'd packed it with if, indeed, it had ever stopped bleeding. And that puffy bruise and split in his scalp above his ear, along with the various scrapes she spotted on his hands, arms, face and through a tear in the knee of his jeans, indicated he'd been in an accident and had lost enough blood to pass out. Unless floating in and out of consciousness had something to do with the wound on his head?

She folded a towel and pressed it against the

wound in his shoulder. He caught his bottom lip between his teeth and moaned at the pressure, the only signs that he was aware of her ministrations as she unrolled a ribbon of gauze and lifted his arm to tie the towel into place. Then she bent his arm and fitted him with a sling made from a dish towel. Since she hadn't seen an exit wound, that meant the bullet was probably still in him. She needed to immobilize the injury as best she could to prevent the projectile from traveling through his body.

By the time she was done, he was breathing more deeply. That was a good sign, right? But he still wasn't opening his eyes and responding to her in any way that indicated he was aware of his surroundings and what she was doing.

Ava gently dabbed at the wound in his scalp, relieved to see that there was no blood coming from his ear, a sign of a skull fracture. She wasn't a doctor, but she'd had basic first-aid training, had endured numerous injuries of her own and was highly suspicious of a concussion. Instead of applying any more pressure to the swelling, she lightly covered it with a gauze pad and activated a chemical ice pack that she placed against the injury, loosely wrapping a towel around his head to keep it in place.

"Come on, mister. I need you to wake up and tell me your name." A cursory search of the pockets of his shirt and the front of his jeans revealed the only clue she had to the man's identity. He had no cell phone with a list of contacts or screen name, but she pulled a ring of keys from his jeans and found a stainless-steel key ring with the same Marine Corps emblem and the initials *L.B.* etched into the polished surface. "L.B.," she read aloud. "L.B.? Hey, L.B.?" she called to him. But clearly it wasn't a nickname he answered to. "Open your eyes, Sergeant? Colonel?" She had no clue what rank a man who appeared to be in his late thirties or early forties would be. But the fact he was military explained the gun and the buzz cut of hair, the mumblings about an extraction team and his ability to hike to her place from wherever the shooting event had occurred. With the mountain and trees reflecting sound for miles, she would have heard shots fired if they'd been anywhere close to her cabin. How much ground had this guy covered?

"Listen up, Marine." She tried another tactic to get a lucid response. "I need your name, rank and serial number." That didn't work, either. She exhaled a frustrated breath, studying the key chain for some other clue that refused to reveal itself before stuffing it back into his pocket. "With my luck, you're probably some Larkin Bonecrusher wannabe."

He moaned again. "Bonecrusher…"

"I need you to do more than repeat everything I say."

Was that a nod? The slight movement of his

head could have been something else, but there
was no mistaking the lines deepening beside his
eyes as he squeezed them tight against a new wave
of pain. *"The Bonecrusher Chronicles,"* he spat
out, fighting to articulate every syllable. "Good
books…"

"You've read my books? *Those* books?" she
hastily corrected.

He was finally communicating in a way that
made sense, and it was on the one topic she didn't
dare talk about.

But even with an addled brain, he hadn't missed
the slip she'd made. "You? You write Bonecrusher…? Sweet. When's the next book…? Why
so long…?"

She went back to work, finding scissors in the
first-aid kit and cutting away the denim around
the cut on his knee and cleaning it. "That's right.
You think I'm the lady who writes the books. You
found me. It's been two years since the last release
and it ended on a cliffhanger between the rebels
and the Fey alliance. You want Larkin and Willow to have sex. You want Maximillia to find a
mate, so the dragon line continues. You want me
to kill off Lord Zeville because nobody likes the
new villain." Ava worked in sharp, sure strokes
as sarcasm leaked into her tone. About the same
time she realized he would need stitches in his leg
and regretted her less than gentle touch, she realized that the man's eyes had opened in slits, and he

was watching her. Lousy timing. Of course, he'd focus in at just the time she was revealing more than she should. Ava ignored his assessing study of her and concentrated on bandaging the cut. "I can't make any of that happen for you. You've wasted your time coming out here. You've got the wrong woman."

"Good books. Buddy put me on to them… last deployment… Willow's hot… Series got me through rehab… Wait." His eyes opened wide and he pushed himself up. "*You* write the books?" But he'd sat up too fast. The color quickly drained from his face. His arms buckled and he swayed.

"Whoa, mister." Ava moved quickly to slide her arms beneath him and catch his shoulders before he struck his head again. "Easy." His head rolled onto her shoulder and his nose nuzzled her neck beneath the collar of her shirt. Suddenly, she had a lapful of man collapsed against her.

One thousand one. One thousand two. One thousand three. Why wasn't she pushing him away?

He was heavier than Maxie's cuddles, but the contact was completely different from the dog's soothing comfort. The shoulder-to-chest contact and scrape of his beard against her neck and collarbone wasn't soothing, but it wasn't completely horrible, either. The urge to shove aside his unexpected touch didn't immediately spike through her, and that should have alarmed her. He smelled of musk and heat from his ordeal, and of something spicy and uniquely male as his short, spiky hair tickled the underside of her jaw. Deployment? Rehab? She smoothed a comforting hand across his clammy forehead and savored the unfamiliar assault on her senses. "What am I going to do with you?"

What *should* she do? Call the sheriff's office? Sheriff Brandon Stout had been one of her childhood friends, a local boy who'd grown up in the area. They'd reconnected every summer when she'd visited, maturing from kids to teenagers. Brandon had been her first kiss during that last summer before she headed off to college at Northwestern. Even then, she'd sensed he'd wanted something more from her, but she had college degrees to earn and had wanted to travel the world and extend her adventures beyond the realm of Wyoming's Wind River Mountains and the Chicago suburbs. She'd made it to forty-two states, ten countries and even the fictional world of Stormhaven before the night she'd been taken from the parking lot outside her campus office and everything had changed. Now she was back in Wyoming, and she knew Brandon would be more than happy if she called and asked him to do her the favor of removing this man from her property.

But she didn't want Brandon to think she wanted something more. She didn't want him to think he was welcome to drop by whenever he wanted. He'd see a phone call from her as an invitation to take their relationship to the next level—to be something more than a friend to her. She needed a friend far more than she needed *something more*. And what she desired more than anything was to be left alone.

Because she couldn't make a mistake then. She couldn't be hurt.

Should she call the volunteer fire department? They'd descend en masse from all corners of the county. She hated crowds of people—there were too many possible threats to keep an eye on.

Maybe she could tell this man to take a hike. Keep the towels, bandages and ice pack. But he was in no shape to send him on his way by himself. And as damaged as she was inside, life had made her fearful, not cruel. She couldn't send an injured man out into the woods on his own to possibly die.

As always, she looked to the clarity and reassurance of the dark, soulful eyes she trusted more than any other. "Maxie, girl—you know what we have to do." The dog tilted her head in that responsive way that made Ava imagine the dog understood what she was saying to her.

She'd already made her scheduled trip into town.

But the thought of this man dying in her arms was even less appealing than facing the friendly people of Pole Axe for a second time this week.

So she scooted out from beneath the man's weight and laid him on the porch before gathering the first-aid supplies and climbing to her feet.

The last thing she needed was an entire platoon of weekend warriors here, looking for their missing buddy—or the sheriff's department and state police swarming the area for a crime scene and asking her questions about a gunshot victim.

Dumping the first-aid supplies and soiled bandages in the kitchen, she pulled a spare blanket from the linen closet, looped the long strap of her bag with her keys and wallet over her neck and shoulder, grabbed the shotgun from inside the door and locked the cabin.

"Maxie? Let's go, girl. Up." Ava marched to her truck and opened the door for the big dog to jump up onto the bench seat. Then she secured the gun in the rack in the back window and turned to find her mystery man had pulled himself up to a sitting position and was leaning heavily against one of the giant ceramic flowerpots at the edge of the porch.

"Maxie's ze dragon in your books…" His eyes were open in slits against the afternoon sun as he nodded toward the dog. "Better 'n a tank for backup…"

Ava hurried back to kneel on the stair in front of him, checking the bandages to make sure they were still in place. "She's not a dragon. That's my dog, Maxie."

"Maximillia Madrona Draconella Reine. Queen Mother of the Dragons."

Yep. He'd read the books, all right. "Come on, Larkin. Can you stand if I help you?"

"I want a pet dragon." He straightened as she sat beside him and draped his uninjured arm over her shoulders, holding tight to his hand and circling her other arm around his waist.

Ava grunted as she pushed to her feet, pulling him up with her. "Maximillia's not a pet. She's a comrade in arms. Part of the team."

He leaned his hip against the railing, gritting his teeth and breathing through his obvious pain. "Dog or the dragon…?"

The man couldn't remember his name. Why couldn't he forget her alter ego?

"Lean on me," she ordered, bracing her legs to take his full weight. "We're going to walk over to my truck, okay?"

He nodded and dropped his foot onto the next step with her before sitting back against the railing. "Where's the rest of my team? Did they make it back to the base?"

Ava tugged at his waist, hooking her fingers around his belt to keep him upright and moving with her. She couldn't be rescuing a welterweight? Still, while she wasn't exactly an Amazon, she wasn't a petite woman, either. And ever since the assault, she'd worked hard to get herself into fighting shape and stay that way. She could do this.

With a little coaxing. "Right now, I'm your team. But you're too big for me to carry, and I don't want to drag you, in case it reopens your shoulder wound."

"Willow, Larkin and Maxie, off on a quest. Jus' like the books." She felt his chest expand against her and his grip tighten on her shoulder as he steeled himself against the pain and dizziness. She had to admire his sheer will and determination as he made it down the stairs and around to the passenger side of the truck with her. "You got a wizard and a thief hidden somewhere? Didn't know I'd stumbled into Stormhaven."

Shaking her head at his refusal to let the story elements of her books go, she propped him against the truck while she opened the door. "You're delirious."

Shielding his head, she got him inside the truck and covered him with the blanket. Ava jogged around the hood and climbed in behind the wheel to start the engine, secure in the knowledge that ninety-five pounds of Great Pyrenees sat between her and the man who had closed his eyes and leaned back against the corner of the seat. She pressed on the accelerator, speeding down the drive as fast as she dared on the gravel.

She turned onto the asphalt road that led past a line of summer homes and rental cabins nestled in the trees against the side of the mountain. Since they were all currently occupied, the fact that he hadn't stumbled onto one of their front porches meant he had come through the wilderness, not from the direction of civilization or even the main highway. But there was nothing in that direction for miles. He certainly wasn't dressed for mountain climbing. Even the dress shirt and what had once been nice jeans weren't what people wore to go hiking unless they were novices. And she had a feeling, judging by that fit, muscular body and those silvery-green eyes that saw more than someone who was dazed and confused should, that this guy wasn't a novice at much of anything.

But he was awfully quiet. Maybe she'd better keep him talking until she got to the clinic and handed him off to the emergency staff. "Hey, mister. You awake over there?"

He was awake.

When she reached the two-lane highway that would take them down the mountain into Pole Axe, she stopped for a black SUV that was moving at a touristy pace up the mountain toward a scenic overlook above the next ridge. The man flinched, groaning at the sudden movement, and hunkered down beneath the blanket.

"Why did you do that?" Ava turned left and followed the blacktop that hugged the curves of the granite slopes, anxious to get the man to the hospital and relieve her conscience of the burden of caring for him. It took him a couple of minutes to sit up straight and lean back against the head-rest again.

"I'm not sure." His slitted eyes were studying the sideview mirror. Ava glanced in the rearview mirror and watched the black vehicle disappear around the bend in the road before he continued. "Something about a black SUV. I wrecked my car."

That explained the blow to the head. Possibly the other cuts and scrapes, depending on how the accident happened. "How do you explain the bullet wound?"

His chin dropped to his chest and he studied the sling and bandage she'd rigged, as if remembering the injury for the first time. "You patched me up?"

She nodded. "You didn't leave me much choice. I couldn't have you dying on my front porch. I'm driving you into town to the emergency clinic. It's a satellite facility from St. John's Health in Jackson."

"Wyoming?"

Poor man. He wasn't even sure of that much? "Yes. I'm driving you down to Pole Axe. We're south of Jackson Hole and Grand Teton and Yel-lowstone National Parks, if that helps."

"Pole Axe," he repeated. "Sounds like a thriv-ing metropolis. I think I'm a long way from where I started this morning."

Was that a clue? Was he recalling his home? "Where did you start this morning?" she asked, slowing to take the next curve. His legs straightened and his right arm shot out, bracing against the dashboard. Odd. "Are you getting carsick?"

Instead of answering, he pulled his limbs back, as though he, too, questioned the instinctive reaction. "I checked out of a hotel room and went to work. Bad day to go."

Although some of the color had returned to his rugged features, he still wasn't making sense. "What hotel? One of the lodges around here? Sounds like you travel for work. Did you drive? Fly into Jackson?"

He considered her questions, although his tight expression made her wonder if concentrating on his missing memories was hurting him. He put a hand on Maxie's back, using the dog's strength to push himself upright and turn toward Ava. She wondered what those eyes looked like when they weren't narrowed in pain and confusion. "Can you tell me my name?"

"I never met you before today."

"You called me Larkin Bonecrusher. That's a fictional name. Why Larkin?"

"Because you're a big bruiser like he is? A warrior? You have an L.B. engraved on your key chain. No wallet or ID on you. Not even a phone. If we were in Chicago, I would think you'd been mugged. I needed to call you something besides 'mister.'"

He released the dog and sank back against the

seat. "Larkin's cool. Got started on those books on my last deployment. Until everything went FUBAR."

Ava frowned at the acronym. "What does FUBAR mean?"

He started to answer, then snapped his mouth shut. "Fouled Up Beyond Any Recognition, Repair or Recall is the polite way to explain it. Suicide bomber made it through a checkpoint. I lost a team of MPs. Busted up my leg. Got sent stateside."

At least some of his ramblings were starting to make sense. "I can tell you're a Marine. Your tattoo and the *Semper Fi* say as much. Are you a veteran? On leave? Do you know where you're stationed?" No answer. "You went to work this morning. Was it a military base? The Air Force is the only branch I know of with a base in Wyoming."

"How did a Marine wind up in the middle of Nowhere, Wyoming?"

Since she had no answer for him, she kept pushing for something to click into place inside his head. "So, you went to work this morning, and everything went FUBAR."

He chuckled, a soft, husky sound that skittered across her eardrums. "You pick up the lingo fast. I'm guessing with these injuries that's pretty accurate."

"Do you answer to Colonel? Gunny?" No response. "General?"

"I wish." There was one fact he knew. He wasn't a general. "Captain. I remember someone calling me that. I'm a captain..." His chin sagged to his chest before he raised it again. "I'm out of the Corps now," he said with a degree of certainty. "My injuries—the leg pain is chronic." He stroked Maxie's fur, as though he found the same calming comfort from the dog as she did. "But I talked to a buddy of mine yesterday who's still in."

"That's great." Ava seized on the flash of memory. "What's his name?"

He swore. "I can't even tell you what we talked about."

"It's okay. You'll figure it out."

"I'm a damn invalid. And I don't like it." He curled his hand into a fist and thumped it against the door, startling Ava and eliciting an alarmed woof from Maxie. "Sorry, girl." He stroked the dog before sinking back into his seat. "I hate being at such a disadvantage."

Ava shrugged, feeling the tension in the truck. Logically, she knew none of his anger was directed at her. But still, she knew enough about violence that seeing others express it could sometimes trigger one of those dreaded flashbacks. Automatically, she reached for Maxie and stroked her fingers through her long hair. The big dog switched allegiances, and they both relished the familiar contact. "I already know more about you than I did twenty minutes ago, Larkin. You're a veteran Marine. You probably haven't been out for too long, judging by that haircut and the fact that you talked to a friend who's still on active duty."

"You called me Larkin again. I like it. It feels familiar." When he inhaled a deep breath to force some of the tension out of him, Ava found herself relaxing a fraction, as well. "I know *The Bonecrusher Chronicles* are fiction, but those are details I can remember. There's a little bit of comfort in knowing my brain isn't complete gelatin." Twisting his body again, he reached over to brush his fingers over the scar on the back of her hand where it still rested on Maxie's back. *One thousand one...*

Oh, hell, no. Ava flinched away and squeezed her grip back around the steering wheel. Even though she'd developed a rule of three with her therapist—allowing someone to touch her for three seconds instead of jumping at even accidental contact—she was already over her quota of human contact today. She couldn't help it. Getting touched without knowing its intent was still a hot button for her.

"Larkin" splayed his fingers apart in a silent apology and pulled away, letting his hand settle into Maxie's fur instead. He scrubbed his knuckles around the dog's ear and beneath her chin, and the big dog leaned into that caress, as well. Maxie seemed to have her own rule of three, four, five, ten—*however long you want to pet me*—where this man was concerned.

Traitor. You're my therapy dog. Not his.

"Sorry," the man apologized. "Didn't mean to startle you. I can see where you get some of your inspiration. Your scars remind me of Willow. She's freakin' hot."

"Scars are not hot."

"She can kick butt. She's royalty, but not a girlie-girl princess. Real woman."

Willow Storm was another member of the Bonecrusher Brigade who used sorcery, swordplay and a team of allies to defeat their enemies and complete their quests. "I'm nothing like her. She's brave and beautiful."

"So are you." If he was waiting for a thank-you for a compliment she didn't believe in, he'd be waiting a long time. He pulled his hand away from Maxie and leaned back against the seat, his eyes drifting shut again. "Glad you didn't shoot me."

"It creates too much paperwork when that happens. Brings too many cops to my front door."

Without opening his eyes, he arched a golden eyebrow and hooked up one corner of his mouth. At least his temporary amnesia didn't impact his ability to understand her sarcasm. "Is that why you're driving me to town instead of calling 9-1-1? You don't like people in uniform? Or is it company, in general, you have an aversion to?"

They passed the road sign indicating they were

within a few miles of their destination. Ignoring his probing questions, Ava tried one more time to help jog his memory. "*The Bonecrusher Chronicles* are fantasy stories. I need you to come back to reality and tell me your name. Why someone shot you. A coworker's name. Anything."

They passed another mile marker before he answered. "I don't remember."

"How did you get to my cabin?"

"Followed the road."

"From where?"

His growing agitation evident in the drumming of his fingers on the armrest, he sat up straighter. "I don't remember."

"Who shot you?"

Whatever amusement he'd enjoyed a moment earlier had faded. "I don't remember." She jumped when he snapped his fingers. "I took Option B."

"Option B? What does that mean?"

"A bullet to the head or rolling off the edge of the cliff. I remember that much. Someone was trying to kill me. I chose Option B."

Rolling off the edge of a cliff? On purpose?

"I'm driving you to the hospital—the clinic we have in Pole Axe. They can do more for you than the first aid I gave you. You've lost a lot of blood. And I'm worried about that head wound. It's probably why you can't recall details. Once the swelling goes down, I'm sure you'll remember everything you need to. Then you can call someone. A friend. Your wife."

He studied his left hand where it hung from the edge of the sling. "No wife." He propped up his wrist and twiddled his fingers in the air, explaining his certainty. "No ring. Not even a tan line where I used to wear one."

"That's hardly definitive proof."

He unhooked his broken utility watch, revealing a distinct pale line on his forearm. "Look at me. I spend a lot of time outdoors." He tucked the watch into his shirt pocket. "Nope. No little woman at home waiting for me."

"Not if you call her the *little woman*."

He chuckled. "I suppose not." His eyes narrowed to slits again. "You're really A. L. Baines? Don't think I didn't catch that slip you made earlier. That's why you chose Larkin instead of Larry or Lance or any other name you could have guessed for me. I've read all your books. You're good."

Yeah. She wrote the *New York Times* bestselling fantasy series.

She was A. L. Baines.

At least, that was the name millions of readers around the world knew her by.

"Baines" came from the Latin root for *bones*, the star of her books. Although the initials had originally been an homage to her parents, Alice and Leo, they had come to represent so much

more. A.L. *Ava. Lives.* Despite one very sick bastard's attempt to keep that from happening. No
one knew her by her pen name here in Wyoming.

"As far as anyone around here knows, I'm Ava
Wallace. That's my real name. If you don't remember anything else about today, remember that."

"Yes, ma'am. Ava Wallace. Keeping secrets."
He seemed to be drifting off again. "You should
be proud of those books."

"I am. But I also need my anonymity."

"Why?"

Too many questions. Ava shook her head. "I
liked you better unconscious."

"You're funny. A little prickly. But funny." His
chest expanded with a deep breath and he sank
farther into the seat. "Why are we keeping secrets?"

Survival. Hopefully, if he let anything slip, the
clinic staff and anyone else they ran into in town
would dismiss it as the ramblings of a man with a
head injury. "Once you tell me your secrets, then
I'll tell you why I need to be Ava Wallace."

"*Need* to be. Interesting choice of words. Deal."
Not really. She intended to be long gone and out
of his life by the time he remembered anything.

He drifted off again. But he was smiling. It soft-
ened his hard, masculine features and made him
almost handsome. Annoyingly so because she
didn't want to be attracted to a man again. Ever.
She certainly didn't want one interested in her.

"Eyes on the road, Willow."

She snapped her gaze back to the windshield. "Ava."

"If I'm Larkin, you're Willow. Dog's the dragon."

"Fine. Go with that when you get to the hospital. They'll call in a psychiatrist." Thankfully, they'd reached the city limit sign with the whopping population of 103, a number that could multiply ten times during tourist season. She slowed her speed to drive the main drag to the clinic on the far side of Pole Axe. "And if you're going to look at me, would you open up your eyes so I know when you're doing it? That whole slitty-eyed stare is a little unnerving."

"Light hurts my eyes." The lone stoplight changed to red and she stomped on the brake. They both jerked against their seat belts and he moaned in pain. "That hurts, too."

"Sorry. I don't mean to hurt you. I…" *Have issues.* Maybe even more than this man who was in such obvious pain and suffering from partial amnesia.

"This is Pole Axe, hmm?"

Thankfully, he hadn't asked her to finish that last sentence. "Just another three blocks and I'll have you at the clinic. I know the doctor there. He'll take good care of you."

"You've taken good care of me, Ava. Despite our rocky introduction. And I'm grateful."

"I hope you'll be okay."

"I hope you will, too. I'm looking at you now, by the way." She glanced across the seat and caught him grinning, despite the effort he was making to keep his eyes open and readable for her. But the grin disappeared as the light changed and she drove through the intersection. "Whatever secrets are haunting those beautiful blue eyes—I hope you'll be okay, too."

Chapter Three

Ava sat in her truck in the farthest corner of the clinic parking lot, playing the voice mail one more time.

"Hey, Ms. Wallace. Detective Charles, Chicago PD, here. Hope you're doing well."

Gabriel Charles had been the first detective on the scene after she'd stumbled into a local trucking office in the warehouse district where she'd been held, and collapsed after her three-day ordeal. He was still the only man she trusted enough on the force to maintain this regular contact with once or twice a month since moving to Wyoming. The man with the gold studs in each earlobe had been supportive and dedicated yet frustrated with her inability to identify the man who'd taken her. She knew her attacker's voice, his general build and the feel of his hands on her body. With her research into weaponry for her books, she'd been able to give Detective Charles a pretty good idea of the different knives he'd used on her. She knew her kidnapper's smell, a pungent blend of garlic, grease and sweat. But she'd never seen his face.

"Sadly, I have to report that there was another

*abduction earlier this month. This guy's been like
clockwork these past five years. Including you,
he's taken someone every summer. Makes me
wonder if he's transient like a truck driver. Or
a tourist who comes to the city to visit family or
see the sights. I'm sorry to share bad news, but
you asked me to keep you in the loop. We found
the woman..."*

Even hearing it for the third time, when the detective hesitated, her stomach cramped with dread.

*"She'd expired. Excessive blood loss. The ME
said one of the stab wounds nicked her heart."*

Ava shook her head, her fingers buried deep
in Maxie's fur. Even if her grip pinched, the dog
didn't shy away from her post. "He's not sloppy
like that." It would end the torture too quickly.
And for the man who had kidnapped her, it had
been all about the torture and the sick release he
got from making his victim suffer, not killing her.
Even now she could hear the moans of satisfaction
he got each time the blade had pierced her skin.
"She must have gotten her blindfold off. Seen his
face."

Or it could be a copycat killer. But she doubted
Detective Charles would call if he suspected that
was the case.

"The MO matches yours and last year's abduction," the detective's message continued. *"I've got
a couple of forensic leads I'm following up on.
You're still my best witness. Hell, you're my only*

witness who's been willing to stay in touch. When we catch him, we'll need you to come back to Chicago and ID him."

When, not if. Detective Charles was always positive that CPD would make an arrest. Or maybe that was the party line to keep survivors like her from giving up hope that they could one day stop greeting visitors with a shotgun and start leading a normal life again.

"As always, if you think of anything else that might help our investigation, give me a call. We'll catch this guy. I promise. Meanwhile, you take care and stay safe—"

Ava screamed at the sharp rap at her window and Maxie jumped up. The dog stepped right onto Ava's lap and barked at the man in the white lab coat. When she recognized Kent Russell, the lone doctor who was working the clinic this weekend, she ordered Maxie back to a sit and rolled down the window. "Sorry about that." She punched off her phone and held it up to explain her reaction. "I was listening to messages. Are you ready for me?"

A toothy smile appeared in the middle of the doctor's curly, salt-and-pepper beard and he lowered the hands he'd raised in apology. "I'm the one who's sorry for startling you. I appreciate you waiting around until we could talk."

Ava breathed deeply, slowing the rapid thumping of her heart against her ribs, before nodding. "I take it 'Larkin' survived?"

The doctor stepped back onto the curb and waited by the landscaping of granite boulders and pine trees that framed the multiuse lot that also served a dentist's office, a chiropractor and an optometry shop in addition to the clinic. "That's one of the things we need to talk about. He's answering to it, but that can't really be his name, is it?"

Ava avoided making any mention of her books and shrugged. "It's a nickname, I guess. I take it he's still a little addled in the head?"

"You could say that. I want to keep him overnight for observation. But he's fighting me on it. Don't know if he's afraid of the cost or getting another shot. Some men can't handle the needles."

Ava tried to picture Larkin backing down from any threat, even one as small as a syringe. "He seems pretty tough to me."

"Sometimes, the tough guys are the biggest babies." Uh, no. She definitely couldn't see the man on her front porch being compared to a baby.

Dr. Russell opened the front of his white lab coat and pulled the pager from the belt of his jeans. He read whatever the message said and tucked it back onto his belt. The Pole Axe clinic couldn't exactly afford cutting-edge technology, so she didn't question his use of a pager. She'd missed Detective Charles's call because there'd been no cell-phone reception inside the hospital itself. Better reception was the excuse she told herself for moving her truck so far from the clinic's sliding front doors. Other people would understand that reason over her desire to hide the fact that Ava Wallace had come to town.

"Physically, your friend only needed outpatient surgery. I removed the bullet and stitched up his shoulder and scalp. Gave him a shot of tetanus and antibiotics, an analgesic for the pain and a blood transfusion. We'd be life-flighting him to Jackson if you hadn't stepped in to stop the bleeding and get him here when you did."

"Thank goodness for my first-aid training."

Dr. Russell scoffed. "You patched him up like a field medic." Coming from a former Army doctor, she supposed that was high praise. "Kept him from going into shock. Probably saved his life."

Ava summoned a smile. The men at that trucking center two years ago had done the same for her before the ambulance and police had arrived. "I'm glad I could help."

"My nurse is moving him to a curtained-off section of the waiting room until we can get a room fixed up for him. Frankly, I'm more worried about the less obvious injuries. X-rays didn't show a skull fracture, but he really needs someone to keep an eye on him the next twenty-four to forty-eight hours. Wish I knew who to call, in case somebody's worried about him."

Kent Russell didn't know her history or her pen name. But as Pole Axe's only full-time doctor, he knew she'd been the victim of an attack before moving to Wyoming. Although she'd started the long healing process with doctors in Chicago, she'd transferred the final stages of reconstructive and cosmetic surgeries to the hospital in Jackson. Dr. Russell had been tasked with changing her bandages and inspecting skin grafts and the newer, less obvious scars for signs of infection as she healed from the procedures.

Ava shrugged. "I'm not sure what else I can tell you. He seems to recall more distant memories, actions rather than names and places. He doesn't remember much about yesterday or today. That will all come back to him, won't it?"

"Possibly. Right now, his brain is like Swiss cheese. He can tell me he's a Marine Corps brat who moved around a lot as a kid, could name bases where they lived, but he doesn't know his parents' names or even if they're still alive." His gaze swept the parking lot beyond her truck before coming back to her. "Could we finish this conversation inside?"

"Sounds like you've already found out more about him than I did." Ava tunneled her fingers beneath the dog's collar. "I need to get Maxie home to exercise her."

And she needed some time alone in the great outdoors to decompress from all the violence and mystery and maleness that had intruded on her life that afternoon.

Another thing she appreciated about Dr. Russell was that he didn't mince words—not about her medical visits, and not about today's events. "Ava. It's a gunshot wound. I had to report it. Sheriff Stout was delayed at the scene of an accident, but I just got word that he's on his way. I don't think you want to have that conversation out here in public. I know how you feel about town gossip. Not that I blame you. If one more of those old biddies tries to set me up with her daughter..."

Ava didn't hear the end of his complaint. She was focusing in the rearview mirror at periodic traffic moving slowly along the main drag, the tourists strolling along the sidewalk window-shopping and the locals who were heading into town for drinks at one of the two bars or dinner at the barbecue joint on Main Street. No sign of Brandon Stout and his official black-and-white SUV. Yet. She needed time to prepare for this meeting. She didn't do well with surprises to begin with, and she'd had far too many unexpected encounters already today.

"Bring the mutt in with you." Dr. Russell brushed his fingers against her arm, quickly pulling away as soon as he had her attention. "I know she's your security blanket. You ought to get a therapy dog vest for Maxie, so no one questions why she's with you 24/7. She's well-trained. Probably wouldn't have any trouble getting certified."

Compliments about Maxie usually made her smile. But she was in more of a panic when she swung her gaze back to Kent's. "You called Brandon?"

Not wasting time on an apology, Dr. Russell continued. "I know you two have history. But he's going to have questions for both of us, and I don't want to report to Stout's office any more than you do. Larkin's not my only patient. It's after-hours and I don't have anyone watching the front desk." He tapped the pager on his belt. "Mr. Garcia's already coded once. I need to stay close by until we can get him stabilized enough to move him to Jackson."

Shaking her head at the inevitability of the reunion vibe Brandon attached to any conversation with her, Ava hooked Maxie's leash to her collar and climbed out of the truck with the dog heeling beside her. Ultimately, she wasn't going to let her trust issues and need for isolation jeopardize someone else's life. Together, they strolled across the nearly empty parking lot. "I'm sorry to hear about Mr. Garcia. He was a friend of my grandfather's. Will he be all right?"

"For an eighty-eight-year-old man, he's holding his own." He opened the automatic door and stood back for Ava to enter the clinic's waiting area ahead of him. "Your friend Larkin has been asking about you."

"He's not my friend."

The doctor chuckled behind her. "Tell *him* that."

Ava tightened her grip on the leash and let Kent pass her to the reception counter. "Has he been… talking about me?" Larkin wouldn't have bragged about meeting her alter ego, would he? She'd made it clear how much she relished her privacy.

Dr. Russell picked up a laptop from the counter and typed in some tidbit of information. "Are you kidding? First, he wanted to know if you've ever shot at someone with that gun of yours. Then he went on about how lucky he was to faint on the right front porch, since you had the knowledge and means to patch him up." He arched an eyebrow and grinned. "He also wanted to know if you were seeing anyone."

"I'm not."

"I suspected as much. But as your local physician, I told him I couldn't reveal that kind of information."

"Thank you."

"I numbed the areas where I gave him stitches. I couldn't risk a normal sedative with that head injury. Although he's physically fit, he's pushed his body to the limit." He inclined his head as the nurse pushed a wheelchair with the very patient they'd been discussing down the hallway. "He'll be out of it for a while. I want to put him to bed and keep him under observation for at least twenty-four, preferably forty-eight, hours."

Larkin's chin rested against his chest and his

eyes were closed. Or maybe he was doing that squint thing again, where it looked like he was asleep, but in reality he was aware of everything and everyone around him. At least his color was better—a healthy tan instead of that blotchy pallor he'd had when he'd been sliding in and out of consciousness. There was a neat white bandage over the gash in his scalp, and they'd changed him from his torn, bloody shirt into a hospital gown with a blanket draped across his lap. The sling that cradled his left arm rested on a plastic bag that held his scuffed boots, socks and folded-up jeans.

Despite her resolve not to have any interest in the enigmatic stranger, Ava's brain couldn't help but note three things. The angles of his rugged face were even more compelling without the blood streaming down the side of his head and matting in his golden beard. His shoulders stretched the thin cotton of the hospital gown to the point it could barely tie behind his neck. And what was he wearing underneath that blanket if he was barefoot and holding his pants? Her palms itched where she clutched Maxie's leash as they remembered how she'd clinically molded her hands over his legs and buttocks when she'd been tending his wounds and searching for ID.

Her observations seemed to heat her blood, making her feel far too aware of the scars marking her face and body, and the emotional inadequacies that were even more crippling. What she might once have embraced as a healthy interest in the opposite sex, the frissons of lusty awareness that bubbled through her veins and fed her imagination with possibilities now made her self-conscious. She twisted her fingers into her ponytail and pulled it over her shoulder, instinctively hiding the most noticeable mark that branded her as a victim—that told the world she was *less*.

Her eyes went out of focus as she dropped her gaze to the clinic's vinyl floor. This was wrong. Being attracted to any man was wrong. Her therapist had said if the right man came along, one day she'd be able to move past her trust issues and form a healthy relationship. But she couldn't trust a man she'd just met. And there was nothing *right* about this Larkin Bonecrusher in the flesh. She only felt this pull toward him because he was hurt, and he'd needed her. The scars and the hang-ups and the big white dog plastered to her side hadn't mattered when he'd collapsed into her lap and huddled against her. She'd been strong enough to be his match in his time of need. She'd been whole enough that he hadn't looked at her with pity or awkward politeness or even fear. He'd simply needed her to be there for him. And no man—no one—had needed her for a very long time. It felt almost…normal. But *normal* was a scary possibility for her. *Normal* had left her life the night she'd stopped to help another stranger.

At least Larkin, as she was coming to think of

him, wasn't afraid to show her his face or let her look him in the eye when she demanded it. And it was such an interesting face...

"No." Ava muttered the admonition, needing to focus on what was important here.

"No?" Kent Russell frowned, looking up from his laptop, not understanding the directive was aimed at herself.

Ava snuffed out that flare of awareness buzzing through her veins and tilted her chin back to Dr. Russell. "Sorry. I had something else on my mind. You do good work, Doctor. He looks a lot better."

"I promise you won't have to be here much longer. I waited until the sheriff called to say he was on his way before I went out to get you." The nurse wheeled Larkin beside a gurney that was already enclosed on two sides by curtains. As the nurse moved the bag from Larkin's lap to the foot of the bed, Dr. Russell tapped something else onto his laptop and then closed it. "If you'll excuse me a minute."

He strode across the waiting area to where the nurse was setting the brakes on the wheelchair and moved in beside Larkin to help him stand. Ava glanced away as the blanket fell to the floor, revealing far more tanned skin down the back of the hospital gown than she was certain Larkin— or anyone—would want to show the world. As the nurse hastily scooped up the blanket and wound it around Larkin's waist, Ava found herself glancing back with a naughty fascination and spotting the distinct line where the tan ended, and a curve of much lighter skin peeked into view.

Feeling the heat creeping up her neck, Ava turned to face the opposite wall. What was wrong with her? True, she hadn't seen a man's seminaked body in several years, but she wasn't a virgin, either. The only man she lusted after these days was the title character of her books. And although they'd shared a few dramatic, life-celebrating kisses, Larkin and Willow had yet to consummate the frustrated desire simmering between them. Ava couldn't bring herself to write that scene. The idea of sex had been perverted by the kidnapper who'd used his power over her to satisfy his own sadistic needs.

However, the tragic incident hadn't killed all sense of longing inside her. Why couldn't she stop noticing and, worse, reacting to the Marine on her doorstep?

Was she transferring her dormant desires onto a manifestation of the fictional hero she'd created?

"Ava?" a deep, husky voice called to her. She held tight to Maxie's leash as she spun toward the man being tucked into the hospital bed. Larkin's eyes opened wide and met hers across the waiting area. He pushed himself up off the pillows and smiled. "You stayed."

Dr. Russell pressed against his patient's uninjured shoulder. "Mr. Larkin, if you could just—"

"Wait." Larkin Bonecrusher pushed back. "I want to see her."

"Close the curtain," Dr. Russell ordered.

"I didn't know she was still here. Ava?" Before the nurse could reach the curtain, Larkin swung his legs off the edge of the bed, banged his stitched-up knee on the wheelchair, then cursed the state of his undress and sat back on the bed. "Why am I so damn groggy? Where are my clothes?"

"Lie down before you fall over."

Larkin rose again, clinging to the edge of the bed, the pleading expression in his eyes sending a message she didn't understand. "Ava? I need you."

Ava shifted on her feet, wondering at the urge to say or do something to calm him down. The instinct to help was almost as powerful as the need to bolt from this place. But the battle between the woman she used to be—the woman who wouldn't hesitate to help someone in distress—and the hypercautious woman she'd become ended abruptly when the outside doors opened again and a man in dusty jeans, wearing a gun and a tan uniform shirt, strode in.

Chapter Four

"Ava! There's my favorite gal." Sheriff Brandon Stout took off his cowboy hat and raked his fingers through his dark, sweaty hair before tossing it onto the reception counter. With the same outstretched motion, he wound his arm around Ava and pulled her into a hug against his stocky chest. He held her so tightly that the corners of the badge pinned above his pocket pinched into her cheek. *One thousand one. One thousand two.* She inhaled a panicked breath, drawing in the smells of smoke and perspiration and something more pungent like gasoline. Ava was mentally suffocating in even this casual embrace. "How are you holdin' up? He didn't hurt you, did he? I checked your truck before I came in. There was blood on the front seat."

One thousand three.

Maxie jumped to her feet as Ava wedged one arm between her and her old friend and shoved at his chest. "Too much, Brandon. We talked about this."

"Right. Your three-second rule." She wasn't sure if that was amusement or irritation, or maybe even pity, in his tone, but he didn't let go. He rubbed his palm in circles at the center of her back. "You must have been terrified. A trespasser, bringing violence right to your front door. You should have called me."

"Brandon!" The tension exploding inside Ava must have traveled right down the leash because Maxie rose on her hind legs, propping her front paws against Brandon's shoulder. The big dog used her full weight to knock the sheriff off balance and give Ava the chance to finally free herself.

"Down, girl." Brandon grinned, pushing the dog off him, and wrestling a bit around her ears to show there were no hard feelings between them. Once the dog had plopped down into a sit between them, Brandon retreated a step, accepting Ava's need for distance, if not necessarily understanding it. "My bad. When I get a call that says 'Ava Wallace' and 'gunshot victim' in the same sentence, I worry."

"I'm fine." Calming herself at the familiarity in his warm brown eyes, Ava even managed a smile. "I was surprised more than anything. I don't get a lot of visitors."

"And whose fault is that?" Brandon had grown a few inches and certainly filled out from the teenager she'd once known, but the boyish smile that had charmed her at seventeen was still evident. Undeterred by the distance or the dog between them, he reached out and tapped his finger beneath her chin. "Always working. My brainy English professor, writing that big dissertation."

Ava glanced over to the curtained-off area, and saw the drape still billowing and the nurse's white clogs returning to the bed as they finally closed off the space and gave Larkin his privacy. Since there were no bare feet in view beneath the curtain, Ava assumed the nurse and Dr. Russell had gotten him back into bed. Good. He needed to rest.

But the tight grip on Ava's stomach hadn't eased. There was so much wrong about this day, so much uncertainty surrounding that stranger that she felt it, too. Was this her empathy kicking in? Was she buying into the whole Willow Storm/Larkin Bonecrusher alliance he seemed to be clinging to? Did she simply want the man who seemed so alone against the world to understand that she hadn't always been such a jumpy, antisocial freak? With that curtain closed, she'd probably seen the last of Larkin, and that was for the best. She didn't need to get any more involved with his trouble. She had enough of her own she was struggling to overcome.

Brandon was still talking, and since there was no one else around, she politely smiled and faced him again. "I'd love to take you out sometime. Give you a break from all that work." He winked. "Say the word, and I'm your man."

Not. Going. To. Happen. The sabbatical story

was the reason she gave anyone around here who bothered to ask why she kept to herself so much. The citizens of Pole Axe thought she was on an extended break from her university in Chicago, needing the quiet time and distance of her grandparents' cabin to conduct her research. She already had her PhD and continued to publish an article here and there. But her books were her bread and butter. She'd earned enough on them that, even if she never finished the seventh one, she could live on what she'd saved and invested. So long as she lived frugally. And other than the calorie-laden specialty coffee she splurged on every Monday at the coffee shop, *frugal* and *hermit* went together. She hadn't gone back to a classroom since the kidnapping. She probably never would. She'd loved teaching. Loved tapping into the creativity of her students and challenging them to create stories of their own. But she couldn't do busy parking lots and campus crowds anymore. She couldn't handle young men with hoodies and downturned faces that masked their expressions gaping back at her from the classroom.

Ava could control her fantasy world. Dragons and great battles, sword fights, curses and noble quests were all safer than the reality of her world back in Chicago—safer than even here in Pole Axe. Maybe if she never finished her book, she'd never have to return to the reality that was so hard for her.

"I wish you lived in town so I could keep a closer eye on you." Brandon caught her hand where she clutched Maxie's leash and squeezed it. "You know how much I care. When Doc Russell said you were involved in this mess…"

"I'm fine. Truly." She squeezed her fingers around his before pulling away. Ava seized upon the acrid odor and smudges of soot and dust clinging to his clothes to distract him from focusing on her any longer. "But you, on the other hand, smell like smoke. Did you trade in your badge and become a firefighter?"

"Oh, that." He swatted at his short sleeves and chest, stirring up a cloud of dust, then frowned and wiped at the streak of grime on his shoulder. But his effort to clean the rusty brown swath of mud and grease only spread the stain onto his chest.

"Stop," Ava chided with a slight smile, grabbing his wrist and pulling it away. "You're making it worse. You need to rinse off that mud and rust?—blood?—then put some pretreatment on it and wash it before the stain sets."

She released him almost as soon as she'd touched him. The man really did need a woman to reel him in and take care of him, but she wasn't volunteering for the job. Still, his smile broadened at even that most practical of attention she paid him.

"Thanks. I'll do that as soon as I chat with our mystery man." He picked up his hat and worked the brim between his hands. "There was a fire at Old Man Harold's junkyard. Nobody hurt. But what looked like a late-model SUV and the cars on either side of it are a total waste. I did what I could to contain it before the VFD got there, but I doubt he's even going to be able to salvage parts. The three vehicles must have been burning for a while before he sobered up enough to crawl out of his recliner and call it in. I'm tempted to cite him for willful destruction of property."

"But if it's his junkyard?"

Brandon could look dead serious when he needed to, and he wasn't joking about this. "We've had plenty of rain this summer. But we're coming up on fire season. I doubt we'll get any more precipitation until snow falls. That fire had ignited the grass. If it got beyond his property line, we might be talking forest fire and I'd be out setting up roadblocks and diverting tourists back into the valley."

"Was it deliberately set?" Why was she asking? Why wasn't she on her way home right now? What curious suspicion kept prolonging this conversation?

Brandon nodded. "An arson investigator will need to confirm my observation, but yeah. There were pour marks. Unless Mr. Harold dropped his bottle of whiskey and a lit cigarette before he went inside and passed out, I'd say somebody set those cars on fire. The perp wanted them burned beyond recognition." He looked over her head toward the curtained-off area and acknowledged Kent Russell joining them at the counter. "That's another reason I want to chat with the guy you brought in."

"You think he had something to do with the fire?"

"He could have been destroying evidence."

Ava hadn't smelled smoke or any kind of flammable liquid on Larkin, the way she had on Brandon's clothes. But a man setting a fire wouldn't stick around to fight it the way Brandon apparently had been battling with the flames and its aftermath. "My place is a good twelve miles from Mr. Harold's junkyard. That's a long way to hike in his condition. You can't place him at the junkyard."

"Not yet." Brandon reached around her to shake Dr. Russell's hand. "Doc."

"Sheriff. I heard about the fire. Is Mr. Harold okay? I'm running out of beds in my clinic."

"That old coot's fine. The volunteer firefighters were still there when I left, making sure there were no stray hotspots. I fixed him a pot of coffee and warned him to drink it instead of the whiskey, or he could lose his whole place next time. He was too far out of it to even notice any trespassers." Brandon directed his smile at Ava. "I go a month dealing with nothing but speeding tickets and running rowdy teenagers home to Mom and Dad— and in one day I get hit with a mysterious fire, a gunshot victim and Ava comin' to town when it ain't even Monday. That, in itself, tells me this guy is trouble. You're sure he didn't hurt you?"

He reached out with one finger to brush aside a tendril of hair that fell over her cheek. Although his indulgent smile never wavered, she saw the exact moment his gaze fell to the scar that bisected her cheek. She felt the hesitation in his touch and did him the favor of turning her head and pulling away. She supposed Brandon still saw her in his mind's eye the way she'd looked twenty years ago, and the imperfections on her skin now were jarring.

Why couldn't he see that she was a different woman from the girl he'd professed to love and move on? "Positive. Any blood you saw in my truck is his, not mine."

"And you've got no idea where he came from or who he is?" She shook her head. Brandon propped his hands at his waist, beside his holstered gun and handcuffs. "We've got a lot of tourists this time of year. Maybe he had a car accident or crossed somebody at Dolan's Bar and got in a fight."

Ava's tolerance for answering questions and pretending she was okay being around so many people was wearing thin. "I really need to get Maxie home. I don't know this man. Can't you leave me out of your investigation? He showed up on my front porch and collapsed. End of story. I don't know anything about burning cars. I didn't hear any gunshots. I'm just the good Samaritan who drove him into town."

Dr. Russell reached into his pocket and pulled out a small, plastic bag. "You're the good Samaritan who saved his life." He handed the bag to Brandon. "Here's the slug I took out of John Doe's shoulder. It's a 9 mil."

Brandon inspected the bloodstained projectile inside the bag before tucking it into the pocket of his jeans. "That's good."

"Good?" The doctor and Ava echoed together.

"Yeah. I was worried you were going to tell me Ava had shot him for coming onto her land. But since she favors buckshot, I can clear her of any suspicion." Had she really been a suspect in Brandon's eyes? Or was this more of his effort to show how well he thought he knew her, and how close he wanted them to be? Her distress must have shown on her face because he winked. "I'm teasin' you, Ave." He finally pulled a pen and notepad from his shirt pocket and jotted some information. "Anything else either of you can tell me?"

"The patient's other injuries are contact wounds," Dr. Russell explained, perhaps even less amused by the teasing than Ava was. "He took a bad fall."

Ava nodded. "He told me he remembered rolling off the edge of a cliff."

"Tumbling down a mountainside would certainly account for the injuries I stitched up. He's lucky he didn't break anything. He's got plenty of bruises, inside and out, though." With a weary sigh, Dr. Russell pulled back the front of his lab coat and hooked his fingers into the pockets of his jeans. "He said his name is Larkin Bonecrusher. What do you make of that?"

Brandon snorted a laugh. "That's an alias if I ever heard one."

"Obviously. But why not come up with John Smith or Bob Jones if he wanted to hide his identity? Bonecrusher is a little dramatic, don't you think?"

"Is he on something? Delusional?"

"I didn't detect any drugs in his system. But he took at least one good blow to the head, so I believe his amnesia is real. Now whether it's permanent, I can't tell you. If he's not lucid in the next twenty-four hours, I'm going to refer him to a neurologist in Jackson. I'd prefer it if you allowed him a good night's sleep before you question him. He might remember more then."

"You know the drill, Doc. Procedure says I've got to talk to him as soon as possible, while his memories are still fresh."

"What memories? My patient needs his rest. Trust me, you'll get better answers in the morning."

"I need answers now. What if I've got a shooter running around my county? Or another accident victim who wasn't as lucky as this guy to see the inside of a hospital?" She felt the focus of both men shift to her. "Ava, did he say anything to you?"

Um, loves my books. Says I have beautiful eyes. Thinks my dog is a dragon. None of which she would share with these two men. "He was in and out of consciousness. Sorry I can't—" She jumped at the beeping of an alarm from the computer behind her.

Kent Russell dashed around the counter and checked the monitor on the desk. "Damn it. Garcia's coding again." He shouted toward the nurse behind the curtain as he ran down the hall. "Leslie! I need the crash cart in Room One. Stat."

The nurse popped through the curtain surrounding Larkin and raced down the hallway after Dr. Russell. The two medical professionals disappeared into separate rooms a few seconds before Leslie pushed the crash cart across the hall as they rushed to save Mr. Garcia's life.

Ava stroked her fingers over the top of Maxie's head. "Poor Mr. Garcia. Does he have any family left in the area?"

But there was no one listening to her concerns. When she turned to see why Brandon hadn't responded, she saw him striding over to the privacy area. With a tug on the leash, Maxie fell into step beside her as she hurried across the room to catch Brandon by the elbow. He'd pulled back the edge of the curtain, but stopped when he saw the battered patient, propped up on the bed, fast asleep. At least, the veteran Marine with the bruised temple and crisp white sling resting atop his chest seemed to be sleeping. His arm and chest moved up and down in deep, even breaths, but she couldn't help but wonder if those silvery-green eyes behind those dark gold lashes were fully aware of being watched. Ava dropped her voice to a whisper and tugged at the sheriff's arm. "What are you doing?"

The long breath that hissed between his teeth spoke of frustration and fatigue. "Realizing that my long day is about to get even longer." He pulled the curtain to again and patted Ava's hand where it rested in the crook of his elbow. "I'm going to have to hang out here until he's able to answer some questions."

"Dr. Russell said he needed to sleep tonight."

He tapped the badge on his chest. "I took an oath to protect this county."

"And the doctor took an oath to protect his patient." Having passed the three-second mark, Ava pulled her hand from his skin and straightened his collar, which had gotten stuck in the muddy mess on his shoulder. "Why don't you go home and clean up, put this shirt in the wash and then come back. By then, maybe Mr... Bonecrusher...will be awake and you'll have better luck. I'm guessing you haven't eaten dinner yet, either."

Brandon grinned. "Is that an invitation?"

"I need to take Maxie for a walk before we hit the road. It's been a while since she's done her business."

"I'll walk you to your truck. I'll come back later when Doc Russell can be here, so he won't accuse me of bullying his patient."

He put his hat on and led the way to the door to open it for her and Maxie. He fell into step beside her as they crossed the nearly deserted parking lot to the pine trees and boulders where she'd parked. The mountain air had cooled a few degrees from when she'd arrived. But the sun was already forming a pinkish-red glow over the peaks of the Wyoming Range to the west. She wasn't going to make it home before dark.

Brandon moved to the back of the truck, where he opened the tailgate to access Maxie's kennel.

"She'll ride up front with me."

"You spoil that dog."

"I know." While Brandon closed the tailgate, Ava pressed her key fob to unlock the door, and reached behind the seat to retrieve a plastic waste bag for the dog. "If you need me to make a formal statement, you can call me."

"I'll do that." When she turned around, she found Brandon blocking the triangle formed by the open door and truck frame. Thank goodness Maxie was there, forcing a bit of distance between them. Had he meant to trap her here? Or was he unaware of his actions and how they affected her?

"Unless you let me take you to lunch tomorrow? I'll get my report typed up, and we could handle the paperwork then. I'd be happy to drive out to get you and—"

"No." She tamped down on the urge to tell him to back out of her personal space. He didn't understand her anxieties, and she didn't have the time, energy or interest in explaining them to him again. "Call me. I can stop by your office on Monday if you need me to sign something." She shook the waste bag in the air, emphasizing that she was ready to focus on other things now besides the upheaval of her day.

"All right. Whatever you say. I've got your number." Although it was obvious he was disappointed by her refusal, Brandon still smiled and leaned in to kiss her. Wondering if she was even interested in remaining friends with a man this thickheaded, Ava turned her head to offer him her cheek. He hesitated at the scar, then kissed her forehead instead. "Good night, Ave."

"Good night."

He finally retreated far enough to allow Maxie to rise to her feet and tug on the leash. Walking the dog wasn't just an excuse for ending the conversation. "Good night, girl." He scuffed his hands around Maxie's ears and patted her flanks. "Enjoy your walk." Finally, he circled around her truck and headed back to his black-and-white SUV. "I'll let you know if I find out anything about this guy."

"Sounds good."

Once he was inside his SUV, Brandon pulled out his cell phone and tucked the hands-free earpiece into his ear, probably calling in his location to his office. His headlights went on as he pulled out of the parking lot, reminding Ava that she needed to get moving. "Come on, Maxie. Let's make this fast."

But, of course, when she wanted to settle for a short walk around the perimeter of the parking lot, Maxie insisted on stretching her legs and sniffing all the town smells that weren't evident in the woods around the cabin where she usually roamed. They stopped at nearly every rock and tree and revisited a couple of them twice. Since Maxie had been such a trouper with the day's unusual events, and had had her back more than once throughout the day, Ava couldn't begrudge the dog the exercise she needed. Even though the sun was setting and their stomachs were grumbling from missing dinner, at least they were alone now. Ava felt her nerves relaxing and the stress of the day melting away beneath her feet. Today had been an anomaly. Tomorrow she could go back to being safe. Isolated. A little bored, perhaps. Frustrated by a book that wouldn't write itself. Emotionally paralyzed and driven into seclusion by a sadistic serial abductor who continued to elude the police. Frozen in a life that no longer seemed to be going anywhere. But safe.

After dropping Maxie's mess into the public trash can and cleaning her hands with a disinfecting wipe from her purse, Ava led Maxie back to her truck. She made her routine safety check underneath the truck and peeked through the windows before she opened the door. "Maxie, up."

While the big dog stretched out across the seat and rested her head on Ava's thigh, Ava buckled up and drove away. Nearly every angled parking slot on Main Street was full, and lights were blazing from Dolan's Bar, the more touristy Cowboy Bar, Buckskin Barbecue, and even Kris DeKamp's Koffee Shop. The newspaper office and Sue Schulman's General Store, full of practical clothes and gear as well as almost any souvenir a tourist could want, were closed for the night. The sheriff's office, volunteer fire department, a small grocery and other local businesses were a block to the east. Farther up the road, and down into the valley in the opposite direction, away from the hub of town, were rental homes, ranches and resort lodges. Some catered to skiing, others offered spa services or outdoor activities or a conference center. Closer to the tree line at the top of the peak was a lodge owned by a company called BDS. Unless they worked there, most of the locals never saw the luxury stone lodge because the best view of the Wind River Mountains and Hoback River Basin came with a steep price.

Ava inhaled a deep breath of the night air coming through her open windows. Music from the bars and voices from open doorways and the sidewalk filled the air as Ava cruised through downtown Pole Axe.

It was a charming town that felt as far away from her life in Chicago as she could get.

She made it through the first stoplight. But when she stopped at the intersection to turn onto the highway, a shadow fell over the ambient light reflecting in her rearview mirror. She looked up, thinking a truck had pulled up behind her. Instead of another vehicle, the shadow was rising right from the back of her truck. Something was moving beneath the tarp that she'd anchored over Maxie's traveling crate. "What the...?"

Everything in Ava tensed. Someone was in the back of her truck. The shadowy figure grew larger, took the shape of a man, vaulted over the side onto the road. The doors were locked. She pushed the button to raise the windows. But the figure was moving forward, not running away.

She eyed the red light. Cursed the cross traffic that wouldn't allow her to stomp on the gas and leave the hitchhiker on the side of the road.

The damn windows were taking too long.

She reached for the glove box where she'd stowed Larkin's handgun, but she cowered back as a strong arm reached over the top of the window, unlocked the door and climbed inside. Maxie pushed to her feet and spun around, filling the cab of the truck. But a hushed command, a gentle touch, and she plopped her butt down beside Ava as the man pulled the blanket she'd used earlier over his shoulders and hunkered down as much as he could between the seat and the dashboard.

Larkin Bonecrusher.

Ava swore as silvery-green eyes bored into hers. "I knew you weren't asleep."

"I can't stay there," he whispered in a tight, deep-pitched voice. His breathing was as noisy and labored as her own, although she suspected for different reasons. Her so-called guard dog stretched out across the seat, content to have him back in the truck.

But Ava saw the real danger. The gun she'd taken off him was clutched in his very capable hand, pointed at her.

She glanced from the barrel of the Springfield Hellcat to the glove compartment and back to those fascinating eyes, which narrowed but never blinked.

"Yeah. I found where you stashed it. I've got the cartridges for that shotgun in my pocket, too." Ava's grip pulsed around the steering wheel. She felt light-headed. Sick to her stomach. This couldn't be happening to her. Again. "When the light changes, drive."

Chapter Five

Every muscle in Larkin's body ached. His brain felt like it was in a fog from whatever the doctor had given him for the pain. His bum leg was screaming at him to untuck from this awkward position, squeezed out of sight between the dashboard and the dragon-size dog. He could feel the chill of his zipper pressed against parts of his body that didn't like to be touched by anything cold. And he felt like a son of a bitch for doing this to Ava.

He'd seen the flare of fear in her eyes when she'd spotted the gun he'd retrieved during this impromptu escape. Even without the weapon, he would have found a way to commandeer her truck and get away from that hospital. His brain might not be running on all cylinders, but his gut was telling him that he wasn't safe there. Her knuckles were white where she gripped the steering wheel, but her jaw was set like stone, and her delicate nostrils flared with every breath. That was anger, not fear. She was probably already plotting his demise, or at least a way to escape. Anger was healthy. He could deal with her being angry at him.

He couldn't deal with being at the mercy of someone knowing more about what had happened to him than he did—and having no clue who his enemy might be. Ava Wallace and her dragon dog were the only safe haven he believed in right now.

Ava's gaze shifted down to the corner of the truck where he crouched. "You're not coming with me."

"Don't look at me," he ordered, making her gaze snap back to the intersection. Her right hand came off the steering wheel to stroke Maxie's coat. That was a coping mechanism he'd seen her use several times today. Well, he was coping the best way he knew how under circumstances he didn't fully understand, too. "Don't let anyone see I'm in here with you. Don't do anything to signal other drivers. You're not in any danger unless you give me up." The glow of the traffic light that tinted the dog's white fur through the windshield changed from red to green. "Drive."

Her foot didn't move off the brake. "Where am I taking you?"

"Your place."

"No." She had both hands back on the steering wheel.

More teddy bear than dragon, Maxie stretched out across the seat, resting her snout on her big paws, close enough to him that she could sniff his face and shoulder without lifting her head. Couldn't Ava see that the dog she trusted so well thought he was okay? Shouldn't that reassure her? "Turn the corner. Go."

Only when bright lights flooded the cab of the truck from the road behind them, indicating they were no longer alone at the intersection, did she flip on her signal and make a left turn. The truck's powerful engine hummed as they picked up speed, merging onto the state highway that zigzagged up the side of the mountain toward her cabin. "You know, I could drive you out to the wilderness and leave you stranded in the middle of nowhere."

"I don't think you will. Gun aside, you're a woman with a heart. Or a conscience at least. You don't want me to get hurt."

"Now who creates fiction?"

While he appreciated her sharp wit, this wasn't the time for playful banter. "Did I read things wrong at the hospital?" The sling he wore made it difficult to push himself into a more comfortable position or avoid the dog's curious nose. It had also made it impossible to load the gun he held on Ava. If he'd had a few more seconds before retrieving the weapon and diving under the tarp in the back of her truck, and the challenge of focusing on completing the task in a moving truck hadn't made his head spin to the point of nausea, then he'd be posing a real threat. But Ava didn't need to know the magazine of bullets was tucked into his back pocket. He hadn't wanted to put her in that kind of danger, anyway. Not when he'd sensed an ally in her. "I thought you were helping me when you sent your sheriff friend home after the doctor and nurse were called away."

"I wasn't aiding and abetting a criminal. I felt sorry for you, thought you needed to rest. I regret that now." He felt the truck slow as they rounded a curve, then pick up speed on a straightaway.

Since he hadn't seen any lights coming through the windows for several minutes now, and their steady climb told him they were headed in the right direction, Larkin moved the gun to the hand at the end of the sling. He used his good arm to nudge the dog up into a sit and push himself onto the seat beside her because his knee couldn't take another second in that cramped position. He allowed himself a couple of deep breaths to let the pain in his battered body dissipate before he buckled himself in. Visually assured that she was driving toward her cabin, he tugged at the strangling neckline of the hospital gown he'd hastily tucked into his jeans, and patted his flat belly to confirm the presence of the medical printout he'd stuffed inside the gown. His left hand was strong enough to maintain control of the gun, although it was no longer pointed at her. "Look, all I'm asking for is a few days of refuge. Your place is isolated, yet you've got good sight lines to see anything coming up the road or out of the woods."

"It's my refuge, not yours. If you didn't have

that gun, I'd be dumping you out on the side of the road."

He lightly touched the side of his head. "There's something…wrong in here. I didn't get shot by accident. I need someplace safe to stay while I get my head on straight. I need time to figure out who shot me. I have a feeling he's coming after me to finish the job, and I don't know who to look for."

Ava shook her head, stirring the long ponytail over her shoulder. "I don't do company. I'm the town recluse. The weird lady with the dog. Ask anyone. I keep to myself."

"The sheriff doesn't know that. He was all over you, and you didn't like it." Her head swiveled toward him, her reaction confirming his suspicions about that relationship. He pointed her attention back to the road as they neared another curve. "You told me not to grab you. I thought it was because I was a stranger. But you've told Sheriff Touchy-Feely that before, haven't you? He doesn't listen."

Her grip tightened, eased, then tightened again. Was she upset because he'd struck a nerve? Or was she plotting an escape? Although Maxie seemed like a gentle giant, was it possible she could order the dog to attack him? Sic the dog on him. Skid to a stop. Shove him out the door and drive away. It was a plan he might try if their situations were reversed and he had what he thought was an armed stranger in his vehicle.

"Brandon is a friend from childhood. We reconnected when I moved back to Pole Axe. He wants to be something more. I'm not interested." So, not hatching a get-rid-of-Larkin plan. But one more reason to back up the instinctive distrust he'd felt toward the sheriff after seeing his actions and eavesdropping on his conversation with Ava and the doctor. "If you're in danger, you can't get much safer than a hospital. You should have stayed there."

He watched another mile marker reflect in the headlights and pass by in the darkness of the night and thick trees rising above the drop-off at the edge of the road. The sense of unease he felt watching the pine trees and guardrail meant something. But he wasn't sure what his subconscious was trying to tell him about this drive any more than he could pinpoint the alarm he'd felt at the hospital. "I felt exposed there. In more ways than one. I had a feeling your sheriff wouldn't listen to what *I* had to say, either. He thinks I'm responsible for setting that fire at the junkyard."

"Are you?" He started to answer, but she already knew his response. "You don't remember."

"The answers are here, Ava, I know it. I need time to figure them out." He seized upon the most likely explanation for the bond he felt toward the frightened, angry woman sitting across from him. "You and Maxie are the only people I know here."

"Maxie's a dog."

He looked into the Pyrenees's soulful dark eyes. "I noticed."

"Earlier, you called her a dragon."

"See? I can tell the difference now. I'm better already, just being with the two of you."

"You're better because Dr. Russell took care of your injuries." He hunkered down behind the dog as they passed an oncoming vehicle. "I don't even know what to call you."

He thought of the key chain engraved with an L.B. tucked into his pocket. "Larkin Bonecrusher will do for now."

"I will not be your Willow Storm."

He pushed himself up straighter as they passed through the darkness again. "No. You're Ava Wallace. You saved my life, so that makes you the closest thing I have to a friend in this town."

"I am not your friend, and I'm not going to be your nursemaid. I'll stop at the next turnaround and call the sheriff."

"Empty threat." He understood that he had a knack for reading people—everyone, that is, but himself. "You don't want to ask that guy for any favors. Whatever he wants from you, it's not mutual, and you're worried that engaging him will send him the wrong message." He tilted his head back to look around Maxie's shoulders. "Or is it that you don't want any man touching you?"

"Now you're some kind of psychic?"

"My eyes work fine. I know what I saw when

he hugged you." He scuffed his palm along the dog's muzzle and scratched beneath her ears. "It took Maximillia here to push him away."

"You and your eyes."

Although he wasn't sure what she meant by that, the dog hadn't been the only one to recognize the flare of panic she'd had when the sheriff had wound his beefy arms around Ava and hugged her tight. "Am I wrong about the sheriff? Hell, if I could have gotten up, I would have stopped him myself."

The nostrils weren't flaring anymore. Her fingers weren't pulsing around the wheel. He was right about the sheriff stomping all over her comfort zone. He prayed that, in his desperate need, he hadn't done the same. "Ava, please. Someone's trying to kill me. I don't know who. I don't know why. But I *know* you're not my enemy."

"How can you be sure?" Her chin pointed up with a stubborn resistance that was more than bravado and unexpectedly sexy. "Maybe I'm the one who shot you."

He couldn't help but smile in admiration of her strength. He tilted his head toward the shotgun anchored in her back window. "You favor that Browning stackbarrel, not a 9 mil." He tamped down on the ill-timed attraction he felt. If she wasn't interested in an old friend with a badge, she wasn't going to be interested in a stranger who'd brought a ton of trouble right to her front door. "You're the only person I'm certain *isn't* the bad guy. You could have shot me and dumped me out in the boonies, and no one would have been the wiser. Hell, I was unconscious on your front porch—you could have smothered me with a pillow. If you wanted me dead, I'd be dead. You wouldn't have worked so hard to save my life. That makes you the only ally I trust right now. Please."

They drove another mile in silence before she answered. "I can't. I'm sorry, Larkin. I'm alone for a reason. You don't understand."

"Then explain it to me."

She shook her head. "I don't wish you any harm. But I can't be your ally. I'll drop you off somewhere. I can turn around and drive you down into Jackson if you're not comfortable with the local cops or medical facility. I can float you a loan if you need money for airfare or a place to stay."

"I don't need more cops. I don't need a hotel full of strangers or to put more distance between me and what I suspect is the scene of the crime somewhere around here. I need to hide out with someone I can trust."

The truck swerved onto the shoulder as she turned to him. "You trust *me*?"

Larkin didn't question the instinctive clench of every muscle as they veered toward the guardrail. "Eyes on the road. The last thing I want to do is crash again."

"Again?" He'd blurted out the word without

thinking. But she'd picked up on the slip. "You were in an accident? *And* you got shot and fell down a mountain?"

Black SUV. Racing down the road. The next curve flying up at him. "They sabotaged my car." The glimmer of the memory played through his head like a TV channel that was out of focus. "That's how they stopped me. They forced me off the road. They wanted something from me."

"Who are *they*? What did they want?"

The channel went dark before he hit upon the answers he needed. "I don't know." He tore at the neckline of the infernal hospital gown and reached inside. He pulled out a folded X-ray printout. He turned on the cab's overhead light and opened the black-and-white image. He held it up to avoid Maxie's shadow and pointed to the small rectangular object below his rib cage. "I'm guessing it has something to do with this."

"You stole that from the hospital?"

"It's *my* x-ray. The doc was checking for internal injuries. He found this instead. Asked me about it. I didn't know what to tell him." Maxie showed an interest in the picture by sniffing it, and Larkin suspected that told the dog about as much as he knew, which wasn't a lot. "The nurse left it in my cubicle when she ran out to help with the other patient."

"What is that little thing in the middle of the picture?"

"Looks like a thumb drive to me."

"What's it doing in your stomach?"

"I'd like to know that myself. Doc Russell gave me something to help it pass smoothly. Still might take a day or two."

"That's gross."

"That's a necessity. I need to know what's on it."

"Maybe you should go back to the hospital until you…get rid of it."

He folded up the printout and tucked it back inside the gown. "If this is what the man who shot me was after, then I don't want to be lying in a public facility with no real security, waiting to pass a key piece of evidence."

"I'm sorry for your trouble, but I don't want to get involved." Although she'd seemed briefly interested in solving the mystery, Ava's shoulders stiffened with a resolute dismissal. "I have issues of my own I have to deal with."

"I can see that." Her hand flew to her cheek, hiding the scar that had already seen some reconstructive surgery. He turned off the overhead light, hating that she thought she had to hide the mark from him. "Not your scars," he explained. "Your reaction to things. Your attachment to this big brute." He smoothed his fingers into the dog's fur, wishing he could test the weight and softness of Ava's ponytail instead. "I can tell Maxie's more than a guard dog to you. Sure, I'm curious about your injuries. I'm human. But I'm not going to pry. You've been hurt. Terribly. You have all the habits of someone with post-traumatic stress. I've been there. A bum leg isn't the only reason I had to leave the Corps."

"You have PTSD?"

"I was a career Marine. My last deployment ended with a literal bang." Before those graphic images could surface, he mentally repeated the mantra some headshrinker on some military base had taught him. *Acknowledge. Compartmentalize. Replace the guilt with a more positive feeling and keep moving forward.* "That's one thing I wish I could forget."

"You remember getting hurt?" she asked, as if that might be a trigger for her.

His was something different. "I remember the team under my command getting blown to bits."

Her hand fell away from her scar. She even brushed a wavy tendril of coffee-colored hair away from that cheek and tucked it behind her ear. The moment she ventured out of her own head, she became open, compassionate, brave. A woman he'd like to get to know. Under different circumstances. "I'm so sorry."

He didn't need pity. He doubted she did, either. "I can tell you're afraid of something. Probably whoever cut you like that." He set the gun down in his lap. Maybe there was a better method than coercion to earn her cooperation. "You've already helped me, just by listening and asking the right questions. I'm trained military police. If we could keep talking like this, triggering some of my memories, I'd be happy to help secure your place while I'm there."

"How do you know you're an MP?"

"Body condition. Reflexes and stamina. Weapons knowledge. An instinct to observe the hell out of the details and people around me." A few distinct memories he wished he didn't have. "I may not remember much about today or yesterday, but I remember serving. Training other men and women under my command. Wearing a uniform." He hesitated at that one vivid memory he couldn't forget. *Compartmentalize. Move on.* "If you still feel threatened, let me help you. In exchange for a place to hide out for a few days."

"No."

"But you *are* afraid of something?"

"Larkin..." She slipped him a glance that revealed...hesitation? Fear? Weariness? But then she turned her eyes to the road again. "I'll drive you anywhere else you want to go. Beyond that, I can't help you."

Coercion—no. Hooking her curiosity—no. Revealing they were both damaged souls—no. Bargaining—no. Hell. He only had one option left to secure her cooperation. "I'll tell everyone in Pole Axe that you're A. L. Baines, famous author, probably rich enough to buy that whole town outright."

"You wouldn't."

"Even if you deny it, just putting the rumor out there in the universe is bound to stir up one or two hundred internet searches on you. I bet you'd have fans coming out of the woodwork."

She released her breath in an audible gasp. "First kidnapping, now blackmail?"

"You leave me no choice. I'm sorry I have to resort to that." If the tattoo wasn't evidence enough, he knew by his scramble to survive and the resolve he felt in making this difficult decision that he was, in fact, a military man. He had a mission to complete, and he needed her on his team to do it. "I won't do anything to hurt you, Ava. But I need an ally, and you're it."

She shook her head. "How can you need someone like me?"

That was self-doubt, not a protest. Something in his heart tugged at the captivating dichotomy of Ava's personality. Strength and vulnerability. Bravery and insecurity. A wildly creative imagination and a stone-cold grasp on reality. A legit talent in the art of sarcasm, and he had yet to hear her laugh. He carefully considered his answer. "Something about you makes me think you know exactly how I'm feeling right now."

"The last time I tried to help a man who needed me..." The truck gained speed as she shot him a sharp look. But she swallowed whatever emotion had darkened her eyes and spilled a truth he hadn't expected to hear. "I was kidnapped two years ago." Guilt, instant and overwhelming, weighed heavier than the gun lying in his lap. "Not like this. He didn't need a gun. I voluntarily went to him. He was lying in a parking lot on campus, next to a beat-up old car. I thought he was a student who was hurt. Then he was smashing my head on the pavement. I woke up in my underwear, blindfolded, cold, strapped to a chair…and he…kept me. For three days, he tortured…" She ended with a blunt, "The scars are all from him."

Shock numbed him for a few moments. "I'm sorry. I had no idea." And then the anger kicked in. He swore. Repeatedly. "And here I am, kidnapping you." Survival had been his only goal. Truth was the key to reaching that goal. Ava Wallace had unwittingly offered him a way to achieve both. But there was a limit to who and what he'd sacrifice to complete his mission—and he'd just reached that limit with her confession. The end hadn't justified the means. There was so much wrong with what she'd shared that Larkin felt like an ass for reaching out to her, for demanding something she couldn't give him—something she shouldn't have to give anyone. Whatever hell had screwed up his day, she'd been through worse and didn't need to be a part of his world. When they sped past a forestry department sign indicating a stopping place up ahead, he pointed to it. "Pull off at that scenic overlook."

The truck wasn't slowing down. "You won't be able to see anything at night."

"I'm not interested in the view. Pull off." He winced against the seat belt as she stomped on the brake to make the turnoff.

Gravel crunched beneath the tires before she pulled into a parking slot facing the sidewalk and low rock wall that probably revealed a picturesque photo op of the lush, tree-covered mountains in the daylight. She shifted into Park and set the brake. "Are you not feeling well?"

Nope. He was suffocating. Suffocating from the weight of guilt at subjecting Ava to any part of his trouble, and frustration that he hadn't seen it coming and he couldn't seem to do a damn thing about it. Except this. He had to tuck the gun into the back of his belt and push the curious dog out of his face to reach his seat belt and free himself.

Maxie, no doubt picking up on the stress that was rolling off him in waves, leaned against his stitched-up shoulder. Larkin grunted at the ache that shot across his chest and down through his arm. But the pain was what he needed to clear his head to coordinate his movements and shove the door open.

"Larkin?"

Another sharp pain jolted through his knee and spiraled up to his brain when his feet hit the pavement. He had to cling to the open door for a few seconds to find his balance. Damn it. Why was he still so dizzy? He was in better shape than this. The day had taken its toll on him, leaving him feeling weak as a puppy. Determination had gotten him through everything else today. His stubborn will would get him through this, too. Once he felt like he could walk without face-planting, he closed the door and headed toward the sidewalk so that the path would be clear for Ava to drive away.

She called to him through the open window. "Where are you going?"

"Away from you." He reached the rock wall, thought he might sit for a moment, then retreated a step at the thought of losing his balance and crashing over the edge of a mountain again. He headed back toward the road instead. He'd thumb down a ride and hitchhike to…somewhere. "It was a mistake to get you involved. I didn't realize how fragile you were. I'll figure this out on my own."

"Fragile?" He could tell from the tone of her voice that she didn't like that. "Is that how you see me? Do you think that's how everyone sees me?"

"Poor choice of words. I meant…" He came back to the passenger window to explain that he was trying—possibly too late—to make things right between them. "You're still working through your trauma. Getting involved with me isn't going to help that." That military resolve to get the job done, no matter the toll it took, faded in the shadows of those striking blue eyes aimed at him. "You saved my life. At the very least, I shouldn't make things worse for you."

Her nostrils flared again, making her look a little pissed. "I'm already involved with you. Get back in the truck."

He pointed to the highway. "I'll hitch a ride with someone else."

"How will you know if the person who picks you up isn't the one who wants you dead?" She waved him back in. "I can handle this."

"Ava, you don't have to prove to me how tough—"

"Get in the damn truck."

He was beginning to see where a lot of her fictional inspiration came from. "That's Willow Storm talking."

"Don't say that. I'm Ava Wallace. I'm a real person. I'm a fighter. I don't...want to be a victim anymore." Her flare of temper faded, and she released the steering wheel to wind her arms around Maxie and bury her face in the dog's shoulder. The stalwart pooch sat up straight, rubbing her head against Ava's, giving her mistress the support she needed.

"Honey, the woman who greeted me with a shotgun and tended my wounds is no victim. The woman who barely batted an eye when I pointed a gun at *her* is no victim." He couldn't tell if she was crying or inhaling deep breaths to get her through the emotions he'd stirred up in her. But he knew he couldn't walk away and leave her feeling raw like this. He waited for the silent sobs to pass and found himself wishing he were in the dog's place, absorbing her tension, allaying her fears, reminding her of her strength. He had one last card he could play to earn her cooperation. But he didn't feel like he was making this deal for himself. When she raised her head again and met his gaze, he made his offer. "Do you think that helping me could aid your healing? Would it prove something to you that you need to believe in?"

"I don't know. I…" She stroked her fingers through Maxie's fur. "I'm tired of being afraid and suspicious all the time. I never used to be. I'm an accomplished woman. I have skills. I've earned three college degrees. Written six books. The last five made the bestseller lists. There's a filmmaker who wants to option the whole series. I have a dissertation and a dozen published articles under my belt. I can handle myself in the outdoors. I'm smart. I'm a good person. I used to help all kinds of people. Cared for my parents when they were sick. Tutored students. Mentored budding authors."

"You sound like a fighter to me to make all that happen."

"I made one wrong decision. Nearly paid for it with my life." She leaned back in her seat, tipping her head back as if sharing her story had exhausted her. "I'm not sure why I'm telling you all this. Why aren't I running over you with my truck and getting away from you as fast as I can?"

"Because you and I get each other. I made a mistake this morning. Nearly paid for it with my life." He repeated her words that rang far too true for him, too. "You're telling me because you understand how that one mistake can change your life. And you'd give anything for a chance to correct that mistake. Maybe I'm that chance."

She nodded. "Nobody here or back in Chicago gets that. People want to take care of me. Or fix things for me."

"Which makes you feel even more like a *fragile* victim."

Yeah, he got that. Even though he'd been tempted to take care of her, too, he could see that that wasn't the kind of help that either of them needed.

"It's another reason I stick to my own company. Then I don't have to see those looks of pity. Even Brandon hesitates when he sees this." She softly brushed her fingers across the scar on her cheek.

Another reason to relegate Sheriff Touchy-Feely to the jerk category, as far as Larkin was concerned. "There's a fine line between compassion and pity."

She agreed. "I can't tell anymore. I haven't been able to trust my instincts since then. That's why there hasn't been another Bonecrusher book. I write and write, but I don't trust that I'm taking the story in the right direction. I live like a hermit because I don't trust people."

"The man who hurt you—was he caught?"

It took her long enough to shake her head that he already knew the horrid, unjust answer.

"Is he here in Wyoming?"

Another headshake. "Chicago. I don't know if he lives there, but he's been there every summer for the past five years. That's where it happened."

"That's why your anonymity is so important to you. You're hiding from him." Larkin turned his head and swore into the night. Then he grabbed the edge of the open window and leaned in, wanting to judge her reaction. "Do I look like him? Remind you of him in any way?"

"You're both men." But her attempt at humor fell flat. Her voice was soft, broken, as she reached for Maxie again. "That's the hell of it. I never saw his face. He kept me blindfolded. Detective Charles, a friend of mine in Chicago PD, thinks he has a lead after a recent attack. I'm not the only woman he's hurt. But apparently, I'm the only survivor who's willing to work with CPD. Try to identify him. By sound. By touch and smell."

"Touch and smell?"

"He…had scars, too. I could feel the puckered skin on his arms and chest when he touched me. He had one on his neck, too." Larkin's hand was curled into a fist, ready to punch someone, when she tried to make light of her suffering again. "If you were a diesel mechanic and had the smells of grease and hot metal on you, I don't think I could have helped you."

Probably another reason why she chose to live in the fresh air of this natural habitat. "And his voice?"

"I'll never forget the things he said to me. The way he said them—as if the scar on his neck had damaged his throat, too. But I wouldn't know him if I passed him on the street."

Sounded a little like a suicide bomber back in the Middle East. The young man who'd driven his delivery truck up to their checkpoint had been little more than a boy. Although his team had begun their routine check of the vehicle, they'd taken a few minutes to chat with the kid because they hadn't seen the imminent threat. Hell of a way to live, not having anyone you could trust—not even herself. "He'll know you before you know him. You don't know who your enemy is."

"I guess that does sound familiar." She sat up straight and studied him. "The only difference between us is that I'm trying to forget my past, while you're trying to remember yours."

"I can't do this to you." As much as this woman's books had gotten him through dark times, and her actions today had saved his life—as much as he was drawn to her wit and honesty and strength—Larkin turned away from Ava and started walking.

"Who's going to help you if I don't?" He stopped at her words. Now, who was trying to convince the other that they should be working together as a team? Larkin turned to find her looking at him. Ava's eyes were as dark as the twilight sky. The dashboard lights twinkled like stars reflected there. Larkin felt the impact of her beauty like a punch to the gut. Yeah, he supposed men like Sheriff Touchy-Feely saw the scars first. Or they overlooked her because she hid her femininity by dressing like a boy in those baggy clothes. But there was a light inside this woman that beamed straight into the murky shadows of his soul and illuminated the foggy nothingness of his memories. "It's not realistic to think I can snap my fingers and go back to the person I used to be. But you…need me…to be that person again."

And who was arguing that they'd be better off apart? "I'm not forcing you to help me, Ava. I'll find another way to get to the truth. I was wrong to threaten blackmail. I won't tell a soul you're A. L. Baines. I'm grateful for all you've done for me." He tapped the door with his palm and retreated a step. "You take care of yourself. Be safe."

He spun around too quickly and swayed. When the black night and black asphalt swirled into one, he grabbed the bed of her truck and leaned against it to steady himself. Ava was out her side of the truck in a second, hurrying around to help balance him. With one hand at his elbow, she steadied him against the side of the truck. When she opened the passenger door to help him inside, he discovered he was a little stronger than he'd been that afternoon and planted his feet and pushed away her steadying hand. "I'm not asking you to get involved with this."

Why the hell would anyone think this woman was weak? She grabbed his belt and turned him toward the opening. Larkin grasped her wrist with his usable hand and pulled her grip loose. When he stepped to the side, she shifted. He settled his hand at the curve of her waist and pushed, but she palmed the center of his chest and pushed back.

"Stop fighting me," she chided. "I don't want to hurt you."

He suspected that even with his aching shoulder, he could lift her off the ground and set her aside. But with his wonky sense of balance they'd probably both end up flat on the pavement. This time when she pushed, his knee buckled, and his hips landed on the edge of the seat. She tumbled into the vee of his legs, the brace of her hand the only thing keeping them from full body contact. Larkin froze, not wanting to frighten her once she realized how close they were.

He didn't want Ava, for even one second, to fear him the way she must have once feared her abductor.

She stared at the hand splayed against his chest, and he wondered if she could feel the heat of that

Julie Miller **113**

touch through the ridiculously thin cotton of his hospital gown the way he could. He wondered if she had any idea that she was close enough for him to inhale the herbal scent of her shampoo on her hair. He wondered if she understood how attracted to her he was.

Her fingertips flexed against the cotton, briefly pressing into the skin and muscle underneath. Even that little pinch was a turn-on for him. Could a blow to the head make a guy this hot for a woman he'd known fewer than twenty-four hours? The nurse at the hospital had been pretty, in a delicate, feminine sort of way, but she hadn't even turned his head. Maybe he was into Ava Wallace because this woman's stories had already filled his imagination, distracted him from months of pain and rehab and touched his soul. She reminded him of the strong and sexy Willow of her books. It felt like he'd known her a lot longer than twenty-four hours.

"Maybe I need someone to ask for my help." He could see the wheels inside her head turning behind her eyes. And then she blinked and turned her face up to his, and he knew he'd agree to whatever deal she had in mind. "I make no guarantees about how much good I'll really be to you. And I can't promise I won't have a panic attack and flip out on you, possibly make things even worse." Her chest expanded with a deep breath. "My instincts tell me that I can trust you, and that I'm the only person who can help you, until you regain your memory. Clearly, you think the same thing."

"Ava…"

Just as he covered her hand with his against his chest, she reached behind him and took the gun from his belt before pulling away. He'd been briefly distracted by feelings and chemistry when he should have been bracing to face the barrel of the gun. Ah, hell. Had this whole conversation been a distraction so that she could regain the upper hand? He wouldn't have protested her right to defend herself. But she tucked the Hellcat into her own belt. "I have a three-second rule."

"Huh?"

"I panic when people touch me, especially when I don't see it coming." A hazard of her ordeal, no doubt. "But when I control the touch, or okay it, I've worked up to keeping it together for three seconds before I have to break contact."

He'd been worried about the gun, while she'd been worried about him touching her. Although he felt like she'd been leaning into him a good deal longer, he respected her directive. "Three seconds. I'll remember that."

"Maxie. Move over." He no longer fought her efforts to help him inside the truck because he didn't want to fight her. "You can stay with me until you can look at that thumb drive, or you regain your memory—whichever comes first."

"Ava—"

She held up a finger to shush him. "I need to be able to do this. I need to be able to trust my instincts again. Yes, I made a mistake that night. But I am not the mistake. I need to believe that again." She closed the door and walked around the truck to get in behind the wheel. "The way I live, it should be fairly easy to keep your presence at my cabin a secret for a few days." She reached over to lock the gun in the glove box before starting the engine. "But I am keeping all the guns and ammo with me. Even the magazine that's in your pocket."

Impressed with her observation skills, he pulled out the rack of bullets and handed it to her. "When did you know the gun wasn't loaded?"

"Just now. I suspected earlier when you held it in your weak hand. But I confirmed it when I felt the weight of it." A blush crept up her neck and warmed her pale skin. "And I may or may not have checked out your backside when you stumbled." He arched an eyebrow. Although he couldn't imagine worse circumstances to launch any kind of relationship between them, it was nice to know he wasn't the only one fighting a little chemistry. "You step one foot out of line, though, and I will shoot you myself," she warned.

"Yes, ma'am. I wouldn't have it any other way." He was smiling as she shifted the truck into gear. "You're strong enough to do this, Ava. I know you are. If I can help you in any way with your situation, I will. I owe you everything."

She pulled back onto the highway. "Just get your memory back."

Chapter Six

Light flickered through the treetops higher up the mountain, sharp and blinding enough that Ava shielded her eyes and looked away. It wasn't the soft glow of the rosy gold sunrise creeping through the forest like a warm fog on the eastern side of the mountain. That flash was harsh and cold. Possibly, the sun was reflecting off the window of a rental cabin or the windshield of a car parked at a scenic overlook. Only, the reflection seemed to be moving. She couldn't tell if it was the swaying of the trees, or the reflection itself that was shifting. Then, as suddenly as it had appeared, the discordant light vanished.

"Aliens," Ava muttered out loud, frowning at the anomaly. If only she could truly dismiss such aberrations in her life so casually. She paused in her morning hike to take a quick assessment of her surroundings. Bird calls. Pine boughs creaking in the wind overhead. Soft splashes of water tumbling over the rocks in Panner's Creek down the bank below her feet. The lodgepole pines and smaller deciduous trees were thick enough on either side of the path to block the sounds of the highway higher up the mountain and any view she had of civilization below her in the valley. These things were all familiar to her.

A flash of light through the trees above her was not.

If she'd only seen the flash once, Ava would have dismissed it as a trick of light and brain-stormed a story about an alien invasion. But she'd spotted that reflection high in the sky twice now. Logically, she knew she wasn't going to run into whoever was behind that periodic flash unless she hooked up her rock-climbing gear and started an ascent up the mountain. But logic had little to do with the sensation crawling over her skin that said she wasn't as alone on her walk this morning as she liked to be.

"Come on, girl. Leave that critter alone. All you're doing is getting wet." Ava whistled to draw Maxie's attention from the frog she'd followed to the edge of the creek. Since they were still on private property, she could let the dog off leash. Seeing the pooch she demanded so much from enjoying her free time gave Ava pleasure, too.

Third flash. Slightly different location.

Was that simply because the angle of the sun changed as it climbed higher into the sky? Or had whatever been making that reflection moved?

And then she heard the hum.

A drone.

Of course. The latest technology for professional and amateur photographers alike. Someone must be trying to get that perfect picture of a sunrise over the mountains. Or maybe it was a geological team, or the forestry department or a conservationist, a scientist mapping out topography or tracking the movement of a flock of birds or herd of mountain goats or...

Tracking?

Ava shivered despite the pleasant morning temperature. She tilted her face to the sky once more. The flashes of light were the drone changing directions, the lens of its camera or another shiny component catching the unfiltered rays of the mountain sunrise.

Ava was in the best shape of her life following two years of physical therapy, fitness training and self-defense classes. She hiked these paths every day and barely broke a sweat. Now, she rubbed her palm over her chest, struggling to catch her breath as the mountain air thinned.

The mountain air hadn't changed in the last thirty seconds. *She* was the one who was making it difficult to breathe.

With such dense tree cover and the relatively steep angle, could whoever be up there see her down here? It wasn't as if she were wearing bright colors in her worn jeans and her grandfather's faded plaid shirt that she'd rolled up to the elbows. She turned back along the trail beside the creek. It was one of many paths she'd followed through these woods over the years. Almost every path led back to her cabin. But surely that was too far away for anyone higher up on the mountain to be tracking *her*.

Not for the first time, she wondered how long the hooded scar-face man had watched her before the night of her abduction. Had choosing her been an impromptu decision? *The lady professor is working late on a Friday night—I can take her.* Or had he been watching her for days, weeks, specifically choosing her as his next victim long before he created the opportunity to strike?

"Breathe, Ava," she coached herself. "They're watching the scenery. Not you." Still, a sudden sense of urgency poured adrenaline into her legs. She needed to get back to the cabin to make sure Larkin was still asleep in the guest bedroom. Still safe, still secret. *She* needed to get back to her security zone before paranoia got the better of her.

Maxie was splashing her big paws in the water, getting ready to jump in after the living toy she'd been playing with. Ava thumped her walking stick down on the dirt path. "Maxie! Come. We need to go." The big dog stopped, raised her spotted head and looked up at Ava. Maybe Ava gave off a unique scent when she started to panic. Maybe Maxie could hear the edgy timbre in her mistress's tone. In one instant, she was playing like an overgrown puppy, and in the next, she was loping up the embankment to lean against Ava's thigh. The dog's weight and warmth snapped Ava out of her spiraling mood. Ava lowered her hand to Maxie's head. "That's my good girl." Reassured that she wasn't alone, that she was safe, Ava hooked the leash to Maxie's collar, and they headed back to the cabin.

Thinking she was being watched could be due to any one of a half dozen upheavals she'd gone through yesterday, from greeting an injured stranger with her shotgun to sharing more details about her kidnapping with Larkin than she'd shared in any one conversation with her therapist over the past two years. Yes, he was a kindred spirit who understood PTSD. Yes, he stirred up desires in her that hadn't responded to any man since her abduction. Not that she was ready to act on those impulses. But even the fact that she was aware of a man, and that she suspected he was aware of her as a woman, had thrown her isolated, well-ordered world into chaos.

She'd agreed to help him because it's what the old Ava would have done, because her isolated, well-ordered world was a lonely place to be— because safe wasn't the same as happy, self-confident or even content. Helping Larkin was the biggest risk she'd taken since her life had been cut to bits two years ago. She had to shake things up or she'd never be free of her frightened, lonely life. She'd never be able to complete her book. She'd never be able to live or love again.

But change was hard. It was scary. Taking that risk with her own Larkin Bonecrusher in the flesh was probably what made her see a drone as a threat and pick up the pace. She reminded herself that she had made the offer to help a wounded veteran regain his memory and true identity. He'd offered to walk away and take his trouble with him. But she'd wrestled him back into her truck and made up the bed in the guest room because she was afraid she'd be making another life-altering mistake if she refused to help and something happened to him.

Willow and Larkin had been reluctant allies in her first book. But by book two they'd forged a tight bond of complementary skills and an unshakable trust that one would always have the other's back. Maybe there was something in the stranger's obsession with her books that spoke to that same need in her. They were stronger as a team. She'd keep him at her cabin for a few days because she'd become an expert at safe and secret. In return, she might learn to believe in herself again—and she might learn that there was someone else in this world who believed in her, too.

She unhooked Maxie when they cleared the trees and chased the dog up onto the porch in a game of tag that left the dog panting, and her a little winded—this time from true exertion, not panic. "You win!" With Maxie thoroughly personified in her imagination, Ava pressed a shushing finger to her lips. "We have to be very quiet, Queen Dragon. Larkin might still be asleep. Our wounded warrior needs his rest."

Maxie cocked her head from side to side, reacting as if she understood the words. But as soon as she unlocked the door, Maxie was all dog, dashing past Ava and heading to the kitchen for a noisy drink from her water bowl.

Ava locked the dead bolt and leaned her walking stick in the corner beside the door. She paused a moment to listen to the stillness inside the cabin. A quick walk through the kitchen revealed the mug and glasses she'd set out for Larkin's morning coffee, milk or orange juice remained untouched. She spotted the light beeping on her answering machine on the landline next to the fridge. Not even a ringing telephone had awakened him, apparently, since no one was moving about the house.

Swallowing the trepidation that always seemed to crop up when she got an unexpected message, she pushed the Play button. "Hey, Ava. Kent Russell here. My patient, Mr. Bonecrusher, left the hospital last night. I know you said you were just the good Samaritan who helped him out, but I was wondering if you knew where he had disappeared to. I really need to find him. Give me a call."

Give him a call? And tell him what? Just how good was she at lying through her teeth and pretending she wasn't harboring his missing patient?

Not answering would only make the doctor call again—or worse, stop by to speak in person. Although he might dismiss any nervous behavior because she was the town eccentric, she needed some time to practice playing dumb before that conversation happened.

In the meantime, she'd better check on said patient. She hurried up the stairs and peeked into the bedroom across from hers.

Pushing the door open without a sound, she tiptoed across the rug to the bed to make sure Larkin was still breathing. Although he'd said Dr. Russell had told him rest wasn't a bad thing, she still felt the old-school concern that a head injury and sleeping for so long meant something was wrong.

There was nothing wrong with the way this man slept.

Ava felt a skitter of awareness chase across her skin that was completely unlike that sense of being watched she'd experienced on her walk. Sometime in the night, Larkin had shed the hospital gown and tossed it onto a chair. He'd rolled over onto his back, pushing the covers down to a precarious position below his belly button and over the points of his hips. She glanced at the floor beside the chair and felt another skitter waking her senses. He'd shed his jeans, too.

Ava studied his exposed chest long enough to make sure it was rising and falling with even, normal breathing. She studied it a bit longer because she hadn't really looked at a man in a long time for any reason other than to assess whether or not he was a threat to her.

This was therapeutic, she reasoned, being able to feel safe indulging her rusty hormones. She made a clinical assessment of Larkin's chest and torso and reached the conclusion that she didn't need to buy him any shirts. The muscular hills and hollows of his shoulders, chest and stomach revealed colorful bruises, a sprinkling of much older scars and some intriguing mileage on her guest. The hair that dusted his chest and narrowed into a straight line that disappeared beneath the top of the sheet was mostly a golden color, mixed with a darker shade of bronze and a few sprinkles of silver, just like the close-cropped hair on his head and the beard that was filling in across his jaw and neck.

She moved closer to touch his forehead and cheek. The skin that had been cool and clammy yesterday afternoon was now a warm, healthy temperature. Without any clothing or injury to impede her view, she studied the ink on his shoulder. The fictional Larkin wore a tattoo that had been branded into him by the first master he'd served before defying his tyrannical rule and joining Willow and her band of rebels fighting to bring rights to all people and the magical creatures of Stormhaven. She suspected the Marine Corps tattoo represented a different kind of loyalty to his comrades and a cause. Touching her fingertips to the dark lines, she wondered at the significance of that date embedded in the stylized links encircling his bicep. She traced the curve of the eagle's head up to the top of his shoulder and over the sharp angle of his clavicle, skirting the crisp white square of gauze taped over his stitches.

A deep-pitched moan hummed in Larkin's throat. She snatched her fingers away and snapped her gaze up to his face to make sure he was truly asleep and not squinting through nearly closed eyes, watching her ogle him like a woman who'd never seen a half-naked man before. Since there was no bemused grin or sudden effort to cover himself, she exhaled a silent breath, relieved to see he was truly resting. He might even wake up remembering his name and who had tried to kill him. That's what she should be thinking about, not her wildly errant hormones. She needed to go. Therapy session over.

Ava grabbed the shopping list he'd made for her off the bedside table, pulled the covers up to his chest and hurried downstairs to retrieve her purse and the dog. Locking the door behind her, she hustled Maxie into the truck and climbed in beside the Great Pyrenees. She wanted to get into town to run Larkin's errands and pick up groceries before it got too crowded with tourists on a Saturday.

With one last glance at the cabin to make sure her temporary roommate was still locked inside, and another glance up the mountain to ensure the flashing lights of the drone hadn't followed her home, she started the engine and headed down the road.

Forty minutes later, Sue Schulman, a lifelong Pole Axe resident who'd outlived two husbands, knew everyone in the county and ran the ironically named Hole in the Wall General Store, was helping Ava gather the items on Larkin's list. After the initial gush of welcome and surprise that Ava had left her remote cabin and come to town on the weekend to shop for new clothes, the older woman with the short, bright white hair had literally shushed herself, unwrapped a rawhide treat for Maxie and proceeded to move around the store to retrieve items and bring them to the front counter where Ava waited. Everything Ava needed, from a disposable cell phone to toiletries, was on the shelves at Sue's. If Larkin had wanted a pair of off-season snowshoes or a lime green foam ax with *Pole Axe, WY* emblazoned on it, she could get him that, too, without ever leaving this warehouse of a store that took up one side of the block between the clinic and the town's second stoplight.

Sue didn't mind Maxie coming into the store along with Ava, and she didn't mind carrying a conversation. With anyone. Not with Ava. Not with the tourists who delighted in her stories about the area's history. Not the locals who remembered her daddy's ranch or went to school with one of her two sons. But the two men in suit jackets and sunglasses who chatted for a few moments at the door before one of them left, made Sue pause for breath.

"I wonder what they want." She laid a stack of men's long-sleeved work shirts on the counter in front of Ava. "You go through these, dear," Sue directed. "They're all the size you asked for and will go with those new jeans. Still don't know why you won't let me put you in a pair of women's pants. Your tomboy casual style simply doesn't show off your shape."

That was the whole idea of dressing the way she did. Drawing attention to herself was the last thing Ava wanted.

The older woman turned her focus back to the man in the suit and frowned. "We won't make a sale off him."

Ava noted the high-school girl walking over to the burly man, who removed his sunglasses and smiled at the teenager as she offered to help him. "Maybe he's lost and stopped in to ask for directions," Ava suggested, although a curious suspicion was tickling the back of her neck. Her reaction could be attributed to her instinctive reaction to strangers. But the only time she'd seen a man with a chest that stocky was Detective Charles when he'd worn a Kevlar vest beneath his shirt the day he'd walked her through the crime scene, from the campus parking lot where she'd been taken to the warehouse district where she'd been released. Either the man at the door was training for a body-building competition, or he was armed beneath that suit jacket. She dropped her voice to a whisper. "Do you know him?"

"I don't think so." Sue tapped a bright pink fingernail against her bottom lip. The older woman had spent her whole life in the area, while Ava had only been a summertime resident, so if anyone could place a face, it was Sue. They watched the dark-haired man strike up a friendly conversation with the teen before pulling his cell phone from inside his jacket and showing the screen to the girl.

"Maybe he does just want directions." Ava picked up a green chambray shirt that reminded her of the color of Larkin's mysterious eyes.

"Ava." Suddenly focused on her again, Sue clicked her tongue in a gentle reprimand and plucked the green shirt from Ava's hands. She pulled out a pink-and-gray plaid instead. "I think it's time you zhush up your look a bit. If I can't get you to wear women's clothes, at least try something a little more feminine. Pink was your grandma Myrna's favorite color." She held the shirt up to Ava's chin and frowned. Then she reached into the stack of men's shirts and pulled out a different one to hold up. "The soft blue, I think. It draws the attention up to your eyes. Away from the marks on your skin."

And just like that, Ava was done with the whole

shopping experience. Not because of Sue's comment—after all, her scars were a part of her she could hardly deny. But because of the rest of the conversation she knew would follow. "The blue is fine. I think I'm finished—"

"I feel like I have to take up Myrna's cause since she's not here to help you. I know you came to Pole Axe runnin' from something—a lot of folks do. Why else would you come to this godforsaken town if you weren't born to it."

"I came to work."

Sue waved off that explanation. "Work, schmerk. It's not right for you to be alone so much. You're never going to get yourself a man staying so far outside of town all by yourself and dressing to hide every pretty thing there is about you. You always look so sad, dear. I remember how bright and funny you are. I know Jim and Myrna would want you to at least make friends your own age." The older woman punctuated the grandmotherly lecture with a sigh and threw her arms around Ava in a tight hug. "They'd be worried about you, too."

She patted the other woman's back. "I'm fine, Sue."

One. Two. The hug wasn't ending. She needed to be able to move.

"I think that cute Sheriff Stout has his eye on you."

Ava felt the panic welling up inside her, constricting her throat, blanking out her thoughts. "I need you to let go..."

Ava didn't know if it was the soft woof of Maxie going on alert, trotting over to Ava's side, or something else going on in the store behind her. But Sue abruptly released her and circled around Ava. Ava turned, as well, to see that the man in the bulky suit jacket had moved over to a couple standing at the rack of souvenir T-shirts. He was chatting them up with an amiable smile and showing them something on his phone screen. When they shook their heads, he moved on to another couple.

"What is that man up to?" Sue traced her finger around her lips, as though making sure her lipstick was still in place. Even through the haze of Ava's mini-episode, she recognized the signs of putting on armor and gearing up for an attack. Not that the septuagenarian was going to physically take on a man twice her size. But this store was her territory, and Sue wasn't afraid to speak her mind to anyone. Thankfully, the sorry state of Ava's social life had been forgotten. "If he starts chasing away my customers..." Sue squeezed Ava's arm. "Will you excuse me, dear?"

With the reprieve, Ava could genuinely smile. "You go ahead."

Ava set the jeans and shirts she wanted with the rest of the items already in her pile on the counter. All that was left on Larkin's list was a package of boxer-briefs, which Ava was more than happy to pick out herself, so that Sue wouldn't give her a sales pitch about lacy bras and silk panties, or feed the rumor mill about some of the more unusual items she was buying. She flagged Monica down, and the teen met her at the counter to check her out.

She was helping the teenager pack her items into two reusable bags when Ava heard a gravelly voice from behind her. "I heard you met a mystery man yesterday."

Ava jumped inside her skin and reached for the reassurance of contact with the dog.

At least the older man with the receding hairline and wire-rimmed glasses had been considerate enough not to touch her. His hands were raised in apology as he moved around to stand beside her. "Oh, dear. I'm sorry, Miss Wallace. I forget how sensitive you are. I didn't mean to startle you."

Last night Larkin had called her *fragile*, and now she was *sensitive*? Add in Sue's mothering and she really needed to work on her reputation around Pole Axe instead of living down to everyone's expectations of her. Willow Storm would be insulted. And frankly, Ava was getting tired of it. Last night's conversation with Larkin had been cathartic. Mentally, she was ready to change, but regrowing her confidence and her faith in the world wasn't going to happen overnight.

But it was going to happen.

Ava fixed a smile on her face for the widower

who ran the local newspaper. "It's all right, Mr. Middleton. I'm working on trying to be more comfortable around other people. Coming to town on a busy Saturday is good practice for me." *This is miserable practice for me, but what else can I say? I'm jumpy about hiding a man at my cabin? I was assaulted by a man who's never been caught, and I think anyone who sneaks up behind me could be that guy?* Better stick to the excuses she'd rehearsed and divert attention from her by saying something "normal." "How are your grandkids?"

The older gentleman smiled as she hit on a favorite topic. "Ginny just got engaged. She's asked me to walk her down the aisle."

"Congratulations. You'll look smashing in a tuxedo."

"Thanks." He leaned in a tad and winked. "Her brothers aren't too thrilled about putting on suits and ties, but they're excited about the wedding, too. It'll be back East where they all live. A year from October. It's going to be quite a production."

Ava took the receipt from Monica and tucked it into her purse. "Do you miss living back in DC?"

"Not really." He slipped his hands into the pockets of his khakis and shrugged. "My blood pressure needed the slower pace of life out here. After losing my son and wife, I was ready for a fresh start. Though I do miss tracking down the leads on an interesting story."

And now they'd come full circle to the reason

the editor and chief reporter for the *County Gaz-etteer* had struck up a conversation with her in the first place. Sly. "And you think a mystery man is an interesting story?"

"You tell me."

Even living on the fringes of town, Ava had heard the story about James Middleton's son, a Navy ensign who'd been killed in a training accident. His wife had died soon after from a prophetic blood clot to her broken heart. Ava understood better than most about how a lifestyle change and relocation could help one recover from an emotional upheaval. But once a newshound, always a newshound, she supposed. After retiring from a career at a metropolitan newspaper covering political intrigue, Congressional committees and Supreme Court rulings, the occasional events to drive tourism and agricultural news here must seem pretty tame. Especially with a paper that only came out once a week. Still, Ava wasn't about to indulge his curiosity.

"There's not much to tell. He stumbled out of the woods, fainted on my front porch. I drove him to the hospital and left as soon as Sheriff Stout took my statement."

"You have no idea what his name is? Where he works?"

Ava looped her purse back around her neck and shoulder. "Sorry."

"My sources say he left the hospital without checking out."

"You have sources in Pole Axe?"

He chuckled. "The town gossips. You know how they love to talk. I've heard everything from this guy being shot in the head to being attacked by a mountain lion. While I imagine the truth lies somewhere in the middle, it sounds to me like he needs to be under a doctor's care. Makes me curious about why the man would wander off from the hospital. What if he's a danger to himself? Collapses again, and no one's around to help? What if he's a danger to someone else?"

Ava got a whiff of a woodsy cologne and cigarette smoke a split second before she heard the man's voice behind her. "You're not talking about this man, are you?"

The advanced warning kept her from gasping out loud. Ava turned to see the big man in the gray suit holding out his cell phone. Thankfully, her eyes were downturned when she saw the image on the screen, or he might have seen a flash of recognition there.

Sue had linked her arm through his to escort him to the counter, steering him away from a group of tourists who'd descended upon the section of Wyoming souvenirs. "This is the woman I was telling you about, Roy." Roy? Sue sure could make friends quickly when she put her mind to it. "Our local heroine, Ava Wallace."

The dark-haired man stuck out a meaty hand. "Nice to meet you, Ms. Wallace. I'm Roy Hauser. Security chief for Bell Design Systems. I've been looking for this man."

She barely touched his fingers as they shook hands. "Who is he?"

"He used to work for BDS. Luke's gone missing."

Luke? Bell Design Systems? Larkin's key chain had an L.B. carved in it. *Luke Bell?* Great. Had the heir to a tech fortune stumbled into her life yesterday? No wonder this man was looking for him.

The older man beside her introduced himself, as well. "I'm James Middleton. I run the local paper." The two men shook hands. "BDS. Isn't that a high-tech company? You have contracts with the military?"

"I'm not at liberty to say, sir." He showed them both the picture on his phone again. "You're sure this isn't the man you met?"

The man in the picture staring back at her was fresh out of the military. He was clean-shaven, and she could see his scalp through the close shave of his hair. But even wide open instead of narrowed in scrutiny, the eyes were unmistakable—silvery-green and piercing in their intensity.

A quiver of excitement stirred in Ava's belly. This man knew Larkin. But she had to respect Larkin's request that no one know he was hiding at her place. As long as he kept her A. L. Baines persona a secret, she would do the same for him. She wondered if anyone gave out acting awards for playing dumb. If people believed she was *sensitive* and *fragile*, maybe they'd believe she was clueless, too. This would be good practice before she called Kent Russell back.

"I don't know." She combed her fingers into her ponytail and made a show of twirling it between her fingers. "The man I saw had a beard and longer hair than that. Plus, he was beat-up from his injuries—bruises and swelling. His face wasn't shaped like that." She studied the image on Roy Hauser's phone, hoping to get a glimpse of any sort of identifying information. But in the split second before he swiped it away, she saw no name with the picture, only a code of numbers and symbols across the bottom of the image. Ava glanced up into Mr. Hauser's brown eyes, the way any normal woman would. "From that picture, it's hard to tell."

"Your sacks are full of men's clothes," he observed, perhaps not buying into her helpless, eccentric persona the way the folks of Pole Axe did. He peeked into the tops of Ava's bags. "You know it's a crime to aid and abet a fugitive."

Ava's head shot up. "Is he a fugitive?"

He grinned. "Well, right now he's just a missing person." He pulled the green chambray shirt from the top of one bag. "The men's clothes?"

Okay. So, she hadn't played dumb enough if this

man was suspicious of her guileless responses. Allowing the irritation she was feeling to rise to the surface, she snatched the shirt from his fingers and stuffed it back into the bag before flicking her collar and patting the baggy fit of her jeans, indicating the clothes were for her.

"Ah. I forget that women are as rugged as the men in this part of the country. Sorry to have bothered you." As he pulled back the front of his jacket to tuck his phone inside, she confirmed that not only was he wearing a protective vest, but there was a gun holstered at his waist.

This man was no fool. And even if he was, he wasn't anyone Ava wanted to mess with. Maybe the gun and vest were standard issue for a security chief at a tech company. But was this the man who had tried to kill Larkin? Or was he a friend who was trying to save him before the would-be killer found him?

Before Ava had to make an excuse to escape any more questions, the other man dashed back into the store. "Roy. I've got the doc in his office at the clinic. He's free to talk for a few minutes."

"Thanks." Roy started after his coworker, then paused and reached inside his jacket before turning back. She was relieved to see that he'd pulled out nothing more dangerous than his wallet. He handed her his business card. "In case you run into that man you rescued again. Or think of anything that might help us." She took the card and tucked it into the pocket of her jeans. Roy handed one to James and Sue, too. "If any of you see him, give me a call." Then he hurried to lead the other man out the door. "Let's go."

Sue helped Ava gather her shopping bags. "What can I do for you today, James?"

The balding man smiled. "You free for lunch?"

Sue winked. "For you, sweetie, I am."

Not one to be caught in the middle of anyone else's budding romance, Ava made a beeline for the door. "That's my cue to leave, too. Thanks!"

"Don't be such a stranger," Sue called after her.

The door was swinging shut behind her as she saw the two men in the black SUV pull out and drive the whole block to turn into the clinic's parking lot. The black SUV wasn't unlike the one Larkin had instinctively recoiled from as it drove past yesterday. Had Roy Hauser and his armed sidekick been searching for Larkin then? What was Larkin's connection to BDS? Were they friends or foes? Or had it simply been a coincidence—a sense of being hunted that had made him duck and hide in her truck yesterday?

And if it was just a coincidence, why did Ava get the sense that someone was now watching her, too?

Although the two security men were headed in the opposite direction from her cabin, she decided it would be smarter not to go straight home. Let them settle in with Kent Russell and that interview before they or anyone else decided to follow her.

After locking her bags inside the truck, Ava tugged on Maxie's leash and crossed the street to Kris DeKamp's Koffee Shop. The moment she pushed open the door, she heard a friendly greeting from the dark-haired woman behind the counter. "Hey, there, stranger. And it isn't even a Monday."

Ava held up the end of Maxie's leash before coming inside. "Do you mind?"

"Not at all. Maxie's always welcome here. I've even got a treat for her." As Maxie trotted up and propped her big paws on the counter, Kris tossed her a crunchy treat. Maybe it was just as well that Ava didn't come into town often. Maxie might become a big tub of lard with all this spoilage. Once the dog was chomping on her treat, Kris wiped off the counter and smiled. "What can I get you?"

Ava read the chalkboard behind the counter for the day's selections, and chose a frothy, chocolate-flavored concoction. She almost ordered a second coffee for Larkin. But if she'd had a close call explaining her sacks full of men's clothes and toiletries, then she'd have an even harder time explaining two drinks for one homebody. Instead, she chose a bag of coffee beans to brew at home. If Larkin felt cheated out of a mocha latte, he'd have to be satisfied with this.

"Digging in for the weekend to work on that

dissertation, I can tell. I don't blame you stocking up on caffeine. This is my own roast. I've added a touch of vanilla and hazelnut, cooler flavors for the summer."

Ava inhaled the heavenly brew before taking a sip. "It's delicious. Thanks, Kris."

While Kris rang up her purchase, the coffee shop owner nodded to the Hole in the Wall across the street. "What is Roy Hauser doing here? I figured we were beneath him and his big-money, high-tech ways here in Pole Axe."

Ava nearly dropped her coffee. But she managed to hang on to the insulated cup and casually say, "I just met him at Sue's place. Do you know him?"

The other woman nodded. "I've catered a couple of luncheons up at the lodge BDS uses when they have imported guests."

"Imported?"

"They do a lot of business with foreign investors. When they come to the US, they like to show their guests the all-American sights like Yellowstone and the Grand Canyon. They use the Ridgerunner Lodge up on top of the mountain. Great views. Luxury rooms. Plenty of privacy, yet easy access to the Jackson Airport and parks." She handed Ava her receipt. "Roy and his people do security checks on anyone they hire to work with their executive staff and investors."

"And Roy checked you out?"

Kris pushed her glasses up on her nose and rolled her eyes. "In more ways than one. He asked me out to dinner. Picked me up and flew me in the BDS jet to Cheyenne."

"Wow."

"Well, it would have been *wow* if the company had been more interesting. He's attractive enough in that manly man kind of way. But I'd have paid my own way just to get a real conversation out of him."

Ava's opinion of the security chief was leaning toward suspicion again. *I'm not at liberty to say* had been his response to Mr. Middleton's question about Larkin's picture and working with the military. "Did you think he was lying to you about something?"

"Yeah, but I couldn't tell you what." Kris handed Ava the bag of coffee beans. "I know Bell Design Systems works with some government stuff, so he can't say much about his work. But I'd have been happy with a story about growing up on the mean streets of the city, fighting to make something of himself until he enlisted in the Army and finally found a family in his comrades in arms."

And Ava thought *she* was the one who made up stories. "Is he a soldier?"

"Roy talked more about the money and perks he got with BDS, and how he worked closely with Gregory Bell, the company's founder and CEO. Like that was supposed to impress me." She eyed the door, as if the burly security chief was headed this way. "He seems like he could be military, doesn't he?"

"I didn't talk to him long enough to know." Ava had automatically turned when Kris's focus had shifted. Fortunately, there was no sign of Hauser, his sidekick or the black SUV. She hid her sigh of relief behind another sip of the decadent coffee. "It's good to chat with you, Kris. Thanks for the coffee."

"Good to see you, too. Feel free to stop in more often."

Ava held her cup up in a friendly salute, then headed back to her truck. She set her coffee in the cup holder and loaded Maxie onto the bench seat. She had completed her mission to buy supplies for Larkin and had engaged in more conversation than she had since moving to Wyoming. Was she getting clues to piece together Larkin's forgotten life? Or was she merely taking in a lot of useless facts that might mean nothing?

She was climbing in behind the wheel when she noticed the flyer tucked beneath her windshield wiper. "What now?"

She stood on the running board to pull the colorful advertisement free and noticed similar pieces of paper had been put on the windshield of every vehicle parked in the downtown area.

"Come to the cookout." A group of local ranchers made some good money every summer taking tourists on a ride in a mock wagon train, culminating in a fireside cookout for dinner. The wagon train had been a staple every summer she could remember. She'd even ridden in a Conestoga wagon and gone to the cookout with her grandparents once herself.

She was smiling at the pleasant memory from her childhood until she turned the flyer over and saw that someone had scrawled a message on it.

I will always find you.

Ava's senses suddenly stopped working. Cotton filled her ears, muting the sounds of traffic and voices on the street. Spots swirled through her vision, her breath locked up in her chest and she was suddenly cold. So cold.

But then adrenaline spiked through her system and she jumped down. She ran to the truck beside hers and pulled off the flyer. No message. She pulled out three more flyers with pictures of a Conestoga wagon and bonfire. Dates. Times. A blur of other printing. But no handwritten words.

Words that shouldn't be here.

Words that could only be meant for her alone.

I will always find you.

If she hadn't felt a cold nose nuzzling her hand at that exact moment, she might have fainted. Or screamed. Instead, she knelt and hugged Maxie tight around the neck, oblivious to the voices of concern, shaking off the hands that tried to help.

"I'm okay," she lied to the disembodied voices

that were worried for her, letting Maxie pull her to her feet. "I have to go." She brushed aside the circle of strangers and friends alike who had rushed over to help her and climbed into the truck right behind the dog.

She started the engine and backed out, barely hearing the tires squealing on the pavement as she stomped on the accelerator. She hadn't had an attack like this in months. She'd pushed herself too hard. Made contact with too many people. That drone this morning had put the idea of being watched in her head, and she'd never really shaken that sense of someone tracking her. She'd dropped her guard and hadn't seen the threat coming. She was having a full-blown panic attack in the middle of Main Street, but she couldn't do a damn thing to stop it.

I will always find you.

Ava wadded up the flyer and tossed it onto the floor of the truck. She needed to get out of here. Needed her sanctuary.

Needed someone who didn't see her as a victim. Now.

Chapter Seven

Larkin heard a vehicle crunching over the gravel road and shot up from the stool in the kitchen where he'd been thumbing through the skinny county phone book, wondering who he could call to locate Ava without giving himself away. He knotted the silky ties of the snug, flowered robe he'd found in the bathroom over his jeans, and picked up the carving knife he'd set within arm's reach on the stone countertop, in case an intruder showed up. He'd prefer his gun—the loaded version—but he could defend himself with a knife if he had to.

When he peeked through the curtains beside the door and saw Ava's pickup pulling up to the house, with Maxie's big, panting snout hanging out the passenger window, he exhaled a sigh of relief. "About damn time, woman."

He paused with his hand on the doorknob. Although he wanted to know why she'd been gone longer than a trip into Pole Axe should take, according to his calculations, and ask if she'd considered the importance of having a backup plan or even a way to contact each other if either one of them got into trouble, he thought better of rushing outside and greeting her with a knife in his hand.

While she unleashed the hound and unloaded several bags from behind the seat, Larkin jogged back to the kitchen to return the knife to the butcher block from where he'd pulled it.

Chances were, he was overreacting to her lengthy absence. She had agreed she'd shop for him today so he could have some clothes that fit and a blessed pair of underpants. She'd told him she rose early to walk the dog and might be out when he got up. But he'd slept in later than he had in years, no doubt a side effect of his injuries and the medications working through his system. The list he'd jotted last night was gone from the bedside table, so he knew she'd come in to see him. He'd been half-aware of her presence as he'd slept—floating around his bed, gentle hands checking his vital signs, tending him in a way that made him feel someone cared. Or maybe that had all been a dream conjured by his jumbled brain.

The ringing telephone had jolted him awake nearly two hours ago. When it became clear that Ava wasn't around to answer, he'd grabbed his jeans and run downstairs to hear a message from Kent Russell, asking on his whereabouts. Was the doctor really that concerned about his recovery? While he was being nosy, he listened to an earlier message from Dr. Russell, and another from Sheriff Stout. Was that why Ava had been gone so long? Had one or the other cornered her in town and pressured her with their suspicions that she knew something she wasn't telling them?

He'd been worried that something had happened to her, and he'd had no way to confirm or disprove his worst suspicions. Even more unsettling had been admitting he'd been worried for himself. Ava Wallace was his lifeline to the world. His best chance at survival. Without her, he was a sitting duck, with no clue who his enemy might be or when that enemy would strike again. He felt guilty enough asking her to help him, to help them both recover from the mistakes that left them feeling so vulnerable and alone.

But even more than the guilt was something unfamiliar twisting around his heart. He'd been worried that she'd wrecked her truck on the twisting drive. Or that Sheriff Touchy-Feely had ignored her boundaries and upset her again. Or that whoever wanted him dead had put two and two together and gone after Ava instead of him.

That's what scared him the most.

He liked Ava Wallace. Liked her big galoot of a dog. He'd admired her talent long before he'd even met her. Her bravery was unquestionable. He loved her sense of humor. He could look into those deep blue eyes all day long and, if he was lucky one day, he hoped to taste those full, sensual lips that so rarely smiled. He'd lost too many people who mattered already. Of all the memories he was certain of, the loss of the men and women who'd served with him, trusted him, had been as close as family, was crystal clear. The fact he could feel that loss so much more viscerally than anything else from his past made him think he didn't form many close attachments to people anymore. But in less than twenty-four hours, he'd made a connection to Ava. And the thought of anyone, anything, hurting her hit him like another bullet to the chest.

So, running to the door, swinging it open to meet her on the porch might be overreacting. But since he wasn't exactly in his right mind at the moment, he wasn't going to argue these instincts where Ava was concerned.

"Where the hell have you been?" he demanded before he could temper the emotion out of his words. The dog lumbered past him, but he scooped two grocery bags out of Ava's arms and blocked her path. "You were gone longer than you said it would take you. I had no way to call you. You couldn't leave a damn note? Why didn't you wake me up? I was worried about you."

"You needed your rest." Her voice sounded used up. She stared at the middle of his chest for a moment, but her gaze never reached his eyes.

Then she shouldered past him and walked into the kitchen, where she set two cloth bags onto the counter. Something was off. Something was way off. Avoiding people was one thing, but the Ava he knew was antisocial with an attitude. This robotic tone and distant focus were something else.

"Ava?" He locked the door and followed her to the kitchen to find her studying the knife block before she pulled out the blade he'd used and reset it into its proper slot. What? No freak-out about the knife after the kidnapping nightmare she'd shared last night? No joke about the robe with the pink flowers that reminded him of his grandma's garden? He preferred a slap across the face for greeting her like such a scary jerk to this spooky quiet. He set the sacks on the center island. "I'm sorry. I shouldn't have jumped on your case like that. I let my uncertainties get the better of me. We don't have a backup plan in case this cabin gets compromised or one of us gets into trouble and needs an Option B to stay safe." He circled the island as she unpacked the groceries and turned to the refrigerator to put them away. He made his voice as gentle as a Marine who was used to giving orders could make it. "I was right to be worried, wasn't I. What's wrong? What's happened?"

No reply. No acknowledgment that he'd even spoken. She unpacked a bag of coffee and a disposable cell phone. She pushed the cell phone across the countertop toward him and turned to put the coffee away in a cabinet. This woman had bossed him around six ways to Sunday, pulled a gun on him and ogled him with an unabashed appreciation he wondered if she was fully aware of. He certainly was. That was the fighter she wanted to be—the fighter he suspected she had once been before tragedy had stolen her trust in the world and her faith in herself. Today, she was slowly, methodically going through the motions as though her brain didn't fully realize what her hands were doing.

And it was killing him.

"Ava, I'm going to touch your arms. Okay?" If he hadn't been studying her so closely, he'd have missed the subtle nod. When she didn't flinch at the cup of his hands around her shoulders, he turned her to face him. He hunched down to study her pale skin and her unfocused eyes. "You drove home like this?"

Instead of offering an explanation, she raised her hand and touched the point of his chin. Her gaze followed her fingers as she rubbed her palm against his jaw and curled her fingertips into his beard and gently tugged. He cooled his body's response to her curious exploration. Whatever was going on, she didn't need it complicated by the punch of desire heating his blood. He lifted his chin to give her access to the side of his neck. And when she slipped her fingertips beneath the edge of the silly robe, he understood that she was touching him in the places she'd said her abductor had had scars.

There were no reassuring words he could offer. She had to discover the truth and believe it for herself that he was no threat to her. Eventually, her shoulders lifted with a weary sigh and she slowly walked into his chest.

Larkin wrapped his arms loosely around her. When she didn't instantly bolt at his touch, he slid one hand up beneath her silky ponytail at the nape of her neck and splayed the fingers of his other hand at the small of her back. *One thousand one.* Even with her arms folded between them, she fit perfectly against him. But she was shaking. He felt her breath come in stuttering gusts against the skin of his chest exposed by this ridiculous outfit he wore. *One thousand two.* Ava was usually a prickly touch-me-not, and now she was melting into him. She nestled her head beneath his chin, some of the long strands of her dark hair tangling with his golden beard. Her fingertips slipped into the front of the robe and she palmed the thumping beat of his heart. Seeking warmth? Taking comfort? Ensuring he was the same man she'd made a dangerous bargain with last night? *One thousand three.*

It took a considerable will to relax his arms and step back.

"You counted to three, didn't you." She tilted her blue eyes to his and he breathed a little easier at the clarity he saw there.

"This is *your* sanctuary. We play by your rules."

Even in that simplest of embraces, several strands of dark hair had come loose from her ponytail and drifted in curly wisps against her eyelashes and cheek. "It's nice to have the option to snuggle in or break contact if I need to. Thank you for understanding."

"You know me—I'm all about Option B." He reached out to capture those stray tendrils of hair and brush them off her cheek. But then he pulled away, despite having discovered an affinity for burying his fingers in the sable-colored silk. "If breaking contact is what you need, then that's what will happen."

"And if I don't want to break contact?"

He swallowed hard at the implication that she might want his touch, that she trusted him with that gift, at least a little. "I'd be game for that." No sense denying his attraction to her. "But no pressure. Like I said—your house, your rules."

She crossed to the center island and picked up the discarded sling that he'd never bothered to put on once his mission had been to locate her. She held it out to him. "You're supposed to wear this."

"And you're supposed to be okay. You're not."

She dropped the sling on the island top and went back to unpacking the groceries. "I wasn't always like this, you know. Tentative. Jumpy. *Fragile.*"

"I didn't think you were. Willow Storm is a passionate woman. And I'm guessing there's a lot of you in Willow." Larkin reached into the sack closest to him and pulled out a carton of milk. "Talk to me, Ava." When he handed her the milk, he held on for a few seconds until she made eye contact again. "Last night you said you wanted to be a fighter. Fight through whatever's hurt you this morning and tell me what happened."

She carried the milk to the fridge before she spoke. "I had a panic attack in the middle of downtown."

"Because of me?"

She shook her head. "Because of this." She pulled a crumpled piece of shiny paper out of the second sack and set it on the counter.

He unfolded the advertisement and read the message. "'I will always find you.'"

She carried the sacks to a crate by the back door and stooped to pet Maxie where she'd stretched out in one of several beds Larkin had noticed around the house. "I don't know how many people saw me. But it's the height of tourist season. They were shocked or feeling sorry for me. It's humiliating to lose control of my senses like that. Even worse is how vulnerable I am when that happens. I couldn't see faces. I heard voices asking if I was okay, and I think someone called 9-1-1, but…" She'd been deprived of her sense of sight when she'd been kidnapped. Losing her ability to focus in on anyone had probably fed her panic. "I had to get out of there. No wonder everyone I know walks on eggshells around me." When the big dog rolled onto her back, Ava obliged by rubbing the dog's tummy. "If Maxie hadn't been there, I don't know what I would have done."

"You would have figured it out. You *did* figure it out because you're here now. You're safe." Her hand paused on Maxie's belly. "Clearly, this note triggered something in you. What does it mean?" Nothing good, he could guess from her seeming need to maintain contact with the dog. Although his instinct was to go to her and offer the same support she got from Maxie, he gave her the space she insisted on. "Honey, I'm so sorry this happened. What do you need from me?"

She rolled to her feet and came back to the counter. "Right now, I need you to go away and leave me alone. And maybe you'd better not call me honey. Here." She tossed him the bags of clothes and finally commented on the robe he'd borrowed. "My grandmother would be honored that you like her robe, but I hardly think the pink peonies are something Bonecrusher would wear. There are towels in the hallway closet if you want to shower."

He looped both bags over his good shoulder, wondering if she had truly recovered from the panic attack, or if this was a brave front meant to keep him at a distance. "If I had on my own underwear right now, this conversation wouldn't be over."

She rewarded him with the shadow of a smile. "I can't share my backstory with a man who has no underwear."

She was back with him and she was okay. But there was definitely something wrong when her gaze slid over to the message on the counter. He'd been serious about trading his military police skills for her protection. Even if that note had nothing to do with him, a panic attack was no joke. If he could do anything to prevent another one, he would. However, he sensed that pushing her to talk to him wasn't going to get him an explanation. He'd best give her what she'd asked for. Distance.

As he backed into the living room, he looked over at Maxie, who'd laid her head on her big paws. "You keep an eye on her, okay?" Then he nodded to Ava. "I'm leaving the dragon to watch your back."

A soft smile rounded her lips a little further. "I'll be fine, Larkin. Go."

One thing Larkin hadn't forgotten from his military training was how to take a five-minute shower. Since he was skipping shaving these days, he was stepping out of the guest bathroom in three. But with his bum shoulder making it difficult to lift his arm over his head, it was taking him five times that long to towel off and get dressed.

That's why he was standing at the foot of the bed in nothing but his briefs and his unhooked jeans hanging low around his hips when he heard a startled, "Oh," from the open doorway.

He spun around to see Ava beating a hasty retreat into the hallway. "Ava?"

"Sorry." She tried to pull the door shut after her, but each hand held a mug and she couldn't grab the knob or the door.

Larkin buttoned his jeans and hurried to catch her. "What's wrong?"

When he reached the doorway, she gaped at his chest, then turned her back to him. "I'm sorry. Your door was open. I thought... I can't seem to stop looking at your naked body. I mean... I keep seeing you without your clothes on. And I'm not looking away." She muttered a curse. "Why am I still talking?"

He laughed at the unintended compliment. "Not the worst thing a woman's ever said to me. Especially for a guy who's a little beat-up around the edges."

When she faced him again, her cheeks were that healthy shade of pink he enjoyed putting there. "That makes you interesting."

And now he was the one blushing. Nice to know the attraction he felt wasn't one-sided. But this was hardly the moment to act on it. Time to move on from any further discussion of his seasoned attributes. The fragrant steam rising from the mugs she held reached his nose and he breathed in the rich, toasty smell. "Is one of those for me?"

She held out a mug, which he gladly accepted. "I saw you hadn't helped yourself to anything in the kitchen. Thought maybe you could use some caffeine."

"Desperately." He breathed in the aroma, then sipped the steaming, revitalizing brew. "Mmm. That's good. Thanks."

After another drink, he carried the mug to the bedside table and set it down so that he could pull on a T-shirt. When it got caught beneath his arm and he groaned at the twisting motion of trying to free it, he suddenly felt an extra pair of hands on his shoulder and back. "Try not to lift your arm." His muscles jumped at the stroke of Ava's hands. There was nothing tentative about her touch. And though he knew she was acting as a nursemaid, there was something about her fingers against his skin that felt familiar…and arousing in an ill-timed, moving-too-fast-for-this-woman way. "Do you want the sling? I can run downstairs and get it," she offered.

Why would he remember her touch when he couldn't come up with his own name? Plus, it was a dangerous sign that he wished she'd been taking *off* his shirt, instead of pulling it down his torso. With his *naked body* removed from her view, he moved away from where her hand lingered on his shoulder, although moving away from Ava was the last thing he wanted to do. "I'm not wearing that thing anymore. Makes me feel like I've got one arm tied behind my back. I think the stitches will hold as long as I don't overdo it."

He drank another sip of coffee before pulling on a pair of socks. When he groaned at the resistance of tugging on his work boots, Ava knelt in front of him to help with that, too. "I pegged you for a black coffee kind of guy. Although I do have sugar, half-and-half and four flavors of creamer if you want."

Yep. A man who couldn't properly dress himself needed to stop thinking about the whole sexual tension thing simmering in his blood. "Straight up will do fine." He took another drink a little too quickly and nearly scalded the roof of his mouth. But it was enough of a metaphoric pinch to pull him back to what was important here. "I've got it. Thanks." He took over tying his own boots while Ava rolled to her feet and retrieved her own mug of coffee. "You ready to talk about that note?"

"How's the rest of you feeling this morning?"

So that would be a no. Fine. She wasn't the only one who needed a few minutes to shake off the feeling that their lives had crashed into each other and were irrevocably changing. "I finally shook that groggy feeling. Makes me wonder what the doc gave me for it to hang on so long. Shoulder and knee are better. Still have a thumb drive in my belly. Head's throbbing, and no, I can't remember my name." Enough stalling. He tied off the second boot and sat up. "I'm worried about you. Something happened in town."

She sank onto the bed beside him, studying the

depths of her coffee a few moments before lifting her gaze to his. "Does the name Luke sound familiar?"

"Luke?" Had someone named Luke sent her that message? Oh. He picked up his key chain from the bedside table. "L.B. Luke… Something… Luke…?" He shook his head and tucked the keys to an unknown home or apartment into his pocket. "Should it?"

"Luke or Lucas Bell, maybe?"

"Bell…" That didn't sound right. Hell, the only name that sounded right to his ears this morning was Larkin. He wasn't forgetting that note or her panic attack, but he'd let her lead the conversation where she needed it to go. "You learned something in town this morning about me?"

"There were two men asking about a missing person named Luke. I spoke to one of them. Roy Hauser?" Nope. That name wasn't clicking anything into place, either. "He's probably in his forties. Dark hair. Muscular build. He had your picture on his phone. Mr. Hauser mentioned the name Luke. He said he's the security chief of Bell Design Systems, and that you used to work for the company. I wonder if you could be a relative. I didn't want to confirm that I knew you until I ran it past you first."

"Used to work for BDS?" Maybe his automatic use of the acronym wasn't a breakthrough. Bell Design Systems was a big enough company that he'd heard of it. They designed technology that the military used. He remembered the BDS logo on software and scanning equipment he'd used. But he had no recollection of working for the company itself. "You're certain it was me he was asking about?"

"The man in the picture looked a lot like you. At least, a version of you. Less scruffy—more military man than medieval warrior. The shop owner and our local newspaper editor were already talking about my mystery man. Hauser must have overheard them and came up to me."

"*Your* mystery man?" There was already gossip around town about them? If the locals had made the connection, it was only a matter of time before the people who'd tried to kill him did, too.

"From yesterday. Nobody knows you're here now. They think you skipped town."

Larkin pushed to his feet, pacing the length of the room. "I don't like that he singled you out. I don't want anyone associating me with you. It puts you in the line of fire."

"I wasn't singled out," she assured him. "He was talking to everyone. They were on their way to see Dr. Russell when they left. Doc Russell has been asking about you, too."

"I know. I heard the messages from him."

"More than one?"

He nodded.

She ran her finger around the edge of her mug,

and he once again felt the kick of a memory of her hands on him. "I lied to Mr. Hauser. I said the picture was different from the man I left at the hospital last night. Should I make up a lie to tell Dr. Russell, too?"

If he was looking for a missing person, he'd be questioning everyone. And he'd be watching for subtle nuances in expression that could give away someone with something to hide. Ava wrote fiction for a living, but was she a convincing liar?

She stood, cradling the warm mug between her hands. "Does any of this sound familiar?"

Larkin was pacing again, fighting to make any bit of this information slide into place. *Option B. Bullet to the head or diving off the edge of a cliff. Lying on the ground, looking up at a gun. And the man holding the gun*...could have been Little Mary Sunshine for all he knew. Larkin swore in frustration. Even if his memory was clear, his vision had been blurred from the head injury.

"Don't try so hard to remember," Ava suggested. "It's like when I'm searching for just the right word to use in a scene, and it won't come to me, no matter how hard I try. Obviously, what you're trying to remember is on a bigger scale, but a lot of times the word that's eluding me comes to me when I stop thinking about it. Like when I'm doing the dishes or walking Maxie."

He grunted a wry laugh. "Got any dishes I can wash?"

That earned a soft smile from Ava. "No. But I will take Maxie for a walk after lunch."

"Do you mind if I tag along?"

"Not at all." The smile vanished and she took another sip of coffee, fortifying herself for her next comment. "I have an Option B in mind for you. In case the cabin is compromised, and you need a place to hide."

"Out in the woods?"

She nodded. "I almost went there this morning instead of coming here."

"Because of the note?"

"There's a place I found when I was a little girl. It's on Grandpa's property, but I never told anyone but him where it was. I've gone there a lot over the years when I needed some quiet time. I wouldn't recommend hanging out there in the winter. But in the summer, it's a pretty sweet hideout."

He could picture her as a little girl, with long pigtails and skinned knees, exploring her grandparents' land. She was probably a bookworm who'd climbed a tree and read for hours. "Sounds pretty special. You sure you want to share it with me?"

"I don't have an Option C for you." The crunch of gravel outside the open windows brought an abrupt end to the conversation. Downstairs, Maxie barked and ran to the front door, her big paws hitting like hoofbeats on the wood floor. Ava crossed to the window to peek through the curtain. "Now what?"

Larkin reached the window half a step behind her. "You expecting visitors?"

"Never." Ava palmed his chest, pushing him away from the window before running past him.

He was tall enough to peer over her head before the curtains closed, spotting the SUV with the circle and badge on its side pulling up to the house. "It's your sheriff friend. Want me to answer it?" Larkin was right behind her, coming down the stairs two at a time.

"You can't." He nearly plowed into her back when she abruptly planted her feet and turned. "You're not here, remember?" She pushed him back toward the stairs, then curled her fingers into the front of his shirt when they heard a vehicle door slam. She tugged hard and changed directions, pushing him through the dining area into the kitchen. "I'll get rid of him, but you need to stay out of sight."

Ava wasn't overpowering him so much as he wasn't fighting her wishes in any way. "I don't like that guy."

"So I gather."

"He doesn't respect you. He's like Lord Zeville. Willow wouldn't put up with the way he treats you."

"We can do a literary analysis later." His boots hit the tile floor of the kitchen and Ava guided him around the center island. "Right now, you can hide in the pantry." She pulled her lips to her teeth and whistled at a shrill enough pitch that Larkin grimaced. "Maxie, come!" Okay, that should not be such a turn-on, but this woman was completely in control of that dog and as powerful as he'd ever seen her. The big white dog came loping in at Ava's command and sat beside her. She centered herself by touching the dog's head before the door closed in Larkin's face. The door swung open again just as quickly, and she tossed in the sling he'd left lying on the island. "I'll keep him outside. You stay put."

He couldn't. He couldn't let Ava face the authorities without any kind of backup. If this was about him, he'd reveal himself and absolve her of any wrongdoing. And if this was about whatever relationship Sheriff Touchy-Feely thought he could force on Ava, then Larkin was going to do something about that, too.

As soon as he heard the front door open and close behind Ava and Maxie, Larkin crept out of the pantry, assessing his options in case he needed to intervene. His gaze landed on the butcher block of knives. He palmed the knife he'd used earlier and edged along the walls. Thank goodness the mountain air was pleasant enough that Ava opened windows instead of running the air. Although he couldn't get a clear sight line from the first floor without giving his presence away, he inched as close as he dared to the dining room window over-looking the porch and listened in.

He heard the clomp of the sheriff's boots on the wood steps. "Ava? I heard you had a freak-out in town. What happened, baby?"

If she'd objected to *honey*, then she was probably seething at *baby*.

Her voice was quiet, but she didn't hesitate to answer. "I figured I'd be hearing from you, Brandon. Did Sue call?"

"Sue and Kris both. They were worried about you. Said you were really upset or having a seizure or something." A third clomp told Larkin that Stout had finally been allowed—or pushed his way—onto the porch. "You never used to be like that, you know, before you came back to town."

This guy didn't know about her PTSD? Did he know how Ava had gotten her scars? Had he ever bothered to ask?

"I guess I overreacted." He heard a pause and figured out the flyer was changing hands. "This was on my truck when I came out of the coffee shop. I don't suppose any of the other flyers in Pole Axe had a personal message like this."

The sheriff took his time reading the note. "Since everybody says you went postal on Main Street, I'm guessing this is a threat and not a love letter."

"It's not a love letter. You know I'm not involved with anyone."

"Not for lack of trying." Did he really think that line would work with her? *Get a clue, pal.* "Somebody been giving you grief? That guy you drove to the hospital yesterday? Doc Russell says he skipped out without leaving a forwarding address. Has he threatened you?"

"Kent Russell? He's called a few times, but he's never threatened me." Wow. Although Larkin couldn't see her face from this position, he had to admire Ava's acting skills. He'd never had the patience to deal with a clueless bimbo who couldn't manage an intelligent conversation.

But Sheriff Touchy-Feely seemed to be eating it up. "Not the doc, baby. That stranger who got you involved in whatever trouble he's in."

"Oh. He's gone?" Could the sheriff not see the intelligence gleaming from the depths of those blue eyes? "I left the hospital right after you and haven't seen him since."

"Sue said you were buying men's clothes."

"I needed new jeans," she answered without missing a beat. "I can't keep wearing Grandpa's things. They're starting to wear out."

"Well, there's something hinky about that guy. Besides stiffing the clinic, I'm wondering if he's involved in something illegal. Running drugs. Hiding out from some other crime. You know, I wonder about that vehicle that was destroyed in Scott Harold's junkyard. First, I thought the old man was being irresponsible. But if Mr. Marine is on the run from someone, he could have torched his SUV to cover his tracks."

"I wouldn't know anything about that."

He nodded. "Of course not. Do you want to come into town? Stay with me for a few days? You could work in my apartment while I'm out huntin' down the bad guys. I could grill dinner on the deck. Give us time to catch up on the old days."

"Thanks for asking, but I'm fine here."

"I want you to be safe."

"I know. Oh." Larkin curled his toes inside his boots at Ava's startled gasp. That lout had grabbed Ava again, and Larkin knew he shouldn't intervene. But if anything Sheriff Stout said or did triggered another panic attack, he'd be out the door right now, turning himself in and doing whatever was necessary to make sure Ava was okay. *One thousand one. One thousand two. Anytime now, buddy, let her go.*

And then Larkin heard a woof. Larkin pressed himself flat against the shiplap as Stout stumbled into view and the Great Pyrenees dropped to her front paws. *Good girl*, Larkin silently praised the dog for pushing the sheriff away from her mistress. The big brute wasn't any kind of killer, but she wasn't letting anybody come between her and her mistress if Ava needed her.

Queen Mother of the Dragons to the rescue.

"I appreciate you looking out for me, Brandon," Ava said. "But I can take care of myself."

"I can see that. Maxie here won't let anybody hurt you." The sheriff petted the dog and then moved out of sight, leaving, he hoped.

"Nope. She won't."

Larkin eased his grip on the knife as he heard heavy boots on the steps.

"Mind if I keep this flyer? Could be one of the high-school kids trying to bully someone else or pull a prank, and they got the wrong truck. I'll double-check your make of truck against others that are registered in the area."

"Let me know if you find out anything, okay? Call," Ava insisted, not encouraging any more visits.

"I'll do that. In the meantime, you take care."

"I will."

The sheriff was back at his SUV, opening the door, when he paused for one last condescending reassurance. "Don't you worry your pretty little head about this, Ave. I'll take care of it for you."

Ava was rubbing her fingers over her unblemished cheek as she locked the door behind her and stalked through the dining room with Maxie at her side. Seriously? Had that guy kissed her? Larkin wasn't so enlightened that his blood didn't boil at the thought of another man touching her in a way he wanted. Ava paused but didn't seem surprised when she saw his position near the window.

"I guess I don't have to repeat anything the

sheriff said. The town thinks I'm crazy, and you're a wanted man."

Once he was certain the sheriff had driven away, Larkin followed her into the kitchen. "I really don't like that guy. He's got no respect for the three-second rule." He returned the knife to the block while she opened the fridge and stared inside. "He took the note, didn't he? Not that we can do anything with evidence like that. Maybe he'll get a print off it and tell you who sent it."

"Maybe it was a practical joke like Brandon suggested." He doubted it. He wasn't dismissing any coincidences until he knew who the enemy was, and that the enemy hadn't now targeted Ava. "Hungry? I can throw together something for lunch."

He watched her pull out a loaf of bread and hug it to her chest. "Hungry for answers. *I will always find you.* What does that mean to you? Does Sheriff Stout know? And don't give me that fragile baby flower answer you gave him."

She didn't. "It was a voice from my past."

"I'm right behind you." He pulled her aside and closed the refrigerator door, giving her arm a quick squeeze before he released her, ignoring the urge to pull her against him again and hold her until that haunted look left her expression. "There are no coincidences in my life right now." Her eyes followed his hands as he took the bread from her and set it on the counter. He didn't mind being patient, but they were having this conversation. "Tell me why the note upset you."

She surprised him by pulling his fingers from the countertop. It wasn't the hug he wanted to give, or even the kiss he was longing to try. But it was contact. She'd initiated it. She was still stroking her thumb inside his palm, making him crazy with even that simplest of contact, and he'd already silently counted to seven. He curled his fingers around hers. If she wanted to hold on to him, he wasn't letting go.

He gently asked the question. "*I will always find you* is significant because...?"

"Because that's the last thing my kidnapper said to me before he let me go."

Chapter Eight

"That's the best he can do?"

Ava hung up the phone with Gabriel Charles. Larkin had gone into full-on Marine investigator mode. He'd wanted her to call the detective in charge of her case and ask certain questions. How much of Ava's case was common knowledge? What kind of security protocols did CPD have in place to protect victim anonymity? What specific leads, if any, did Gabriel have on her kidnapper—and were they anywhere close to finding the guy and making an arrest? Was there any way in hell this bastard had made his way to Wyoming to come after Ava again?

The news hadn't been great.

Even though he'd listened to the call via speakerphone, Ava had sensed more than once that Larkin wanted to snatch up her cell to conduct the interrogation himself. Instead, he had to settle for pacing a circle around her kitchen, giving her hand signals she didn't always catch and scribbling follow-up questions on the notepad where she was jotting down Detective Charles's answers.

Ava imagined Captain Mystery Marine had

been an intimidating officer and investigator when he had all his faculties and his body was at one hundred percent. He was intimidating enough as is, with his chiseled, battered body, his golden-bronze beard masking half of his face and those deceptively slitted eyes that saw far more than he let on.

Pace to the window, peek through the curtain. Pace to the back door, scrub his hand over Maxie's head. Return to look over Ava's shoulder, decide he was standing too close for her comfort, then back away and resume his circle around the kitchen again.

Pushing to her feet off the stool where she'd sat, Ava tucked her phone in her pocket. "Detective Charles is as angry as you and I are to find that someone sent me that note."

Larkin propped his hands at his waist. "Am I the only one who feels the clock ticking here? You said no one but you and Detective Charles knew what your kidnapper said to you. You're sure you trust this guy?"

"Yes." As much as she could trust anybody. She went to the fridge to pull out two bottles of water. One of them already had too much coffee in his system. "At least he confirmed that Brandon didn't request the police report about my kidnapping."

"Not exactly. He confirmed that Stout didn't request your information through standard channels." He twisted the cap off the bottle she handed him and took a quick drink. "That doesn't mean Sheriff Touchy-Feely didn't access information about you by other means." He reached across the island to take her hand, the way any normal person who wanted to offer comfort might. But at the last second, he pulled back to toy with the bottle's plastic cap. Ava was at once touched by his consideration of her boundaries and disappointed to realize that she'd scared off the one man she didn't seem to mind being close to. "Either your kidnapper has found you here in Wyoming, or the people after me have accessed those files because they think you're the best lead to finding me. I don't like either scenario." He squeezed the innocent plastic in his fist. "I'm torn between wanting to stay here and protect you, and wanting to run as far away from you as I can and take the threat with me. But if this is about you, then I'd be leaving you alone and vulnerable."

Wouldn't be the first time. Though now she was wondering if *alone* was as safe as she'd thought.

"Where would you run?" she asked quietly. "You said I was the only ally you could trust. Plus, you have no vehicle, no driver's license—and no money. I'll float you a loan if you think it would help—"

"No." Apparently, that offer wasn't up for discussion. "With everything else I'm demanding of you, I will not take your money."

"This agreement is mutually beneficial, remember?" It didn't hurt to remind herself of what she was getting out of helping Larkin, too. "I'm proving to myself that I'm strong and normal and capable of being more than a shadow of who I used to be."

"That was before you got that threat from your past." He forced the lid back onto the bottle and exhaled his frustration. "We don't have a lot of options, do we?"

"We'll think of something. Larkin and Willow always do."

He grunted a sound she was learning was his wry laugh. "I thought you wanted to be Ava, not Willow."

She moved to her desk in the living room and brushed her fingers across her unopened laptop. Typically, escaping into her fantasy world was a reprieve for her. But she hadn't written anything substantial for weeks now. Her brain had been too full of fear and self-doubt to do more than write endless narrative descriptions and battle scenes, edit until there was no voice or heart left on the pages, then write the scenes again. She'd been afraid to invest her emotions into the story. Pulling her hand away, she plucked her last book off the shelf behind her desk. "Willow's not such a bad gal. I just haven't felt much like her lately."

"Do we need to have that conversation again? About where Willow's strength and ability to survive come from? You're probably more capable now than you were two years ago." He came to stand beside her, and Ava breathed in the spicy scent that came off the heat of his skin. Had Larkin simply come along at the time when she was ready to notice a man again? Or did this visceral reaction to the look, feel, sound and, apparently, the smell of him mean something more profound? "You may be different. But you're not weaker. You're not *less* than you were before the kidnapping."

"That's what my therapist says."

"Smart woman."

Ava tipped her head up. "How do you know she's a…?" Ah, yes. Narrowed eyes. All-seeing. "You figured I wouldn't be comfortable talking to a man."

He grinned. "I guess I'm the exception. And I don't have to know my own name to remember how to observe the details and piece clues together."

Ava conceded that his skills hadn't diminished, despite the gaps in his memory. "Besides dealing with the hooded man's threat again, I'm concerned about my pseudonym being leaked to the public. Detective Charles never told anyone, not even within his department, that I'm A. L. Baines. I can see it now. Wealthy, World-Famous Author Gets Kidnapped."

"That would cause one hell of a scandal if that

headline ever hit the news. Is Detective Charles certain that your kidnapping has nothing to do with you being 'wealthy and world-famous'?"

"He ran that angle into the ground more than once." There hadn't been any disturbing fan letters leading up to the abduction. And during the nearly seventy-two hours she'd been held, her kidnapper had never mentioned the books or characters. "The man who took me wasn't insisting I write a story in a certain way or resurrect a dead character. There was never any ransom demand. It wasn't about the books or the money." There was only the slide of his puckered skin against her own, the acrid, oily smell clinging to his clothes and that gravelly voice rasping against her ear. *"Scream for me, darlin'. Bleed for me. That's it."* And then a blade would pierce her skin like a hot poker. His nose would tease the edge of her blindfold as he lapped up the tears that ran down her cheeks, and his fetid breath would quicken with the throes of his sick rapture. She screamed for him. She screamed.

"Ava?" She heard a crash through the stuffing in her ears. Larkin's bronze beard swam through her vision. There was a shrill whistle and a sharp command. "Maxie!"

For a moment, Ava thought she was falling. She hit a wall at her back and floated gently downward as her knees buckled.

"I've got you." A familiar weight leaned against her, and she was momentarily cocooned between two warm, immovable objects. "Do your thing, girl."

When Ava's senses gradually returned, she was sitting on the floor. Her face was pressed against the warmth of Maxie's fur and someone was holding her arms around the dog's neck, splaying her fingers through the dog's soft coat.

"Good girl, Maxie." Larkin's voice was a deep-pitched vibration that cut through the fog of the flashback. "That's it, Queen Dragon. You take care of our Willow. Do your magic."

"Larkin?" Ava whispered, orienting herself to her surroundings. Home. Maxie. An open book beside her overturned desk chair.

Silvery-green eyes looking down into hers. "You okay? You with me?"

Ava nodded. She petted Maxie around the ears and discovered she wasn't the only one praising the dog. But when her fingers brushed against Larkin's, he sat back on the rug, facing her with the dog between them.

"I'm sorry. I made you go to a place I never meant to. You faded away from me." The lines on his face were harsh with regret. "I'm sorry if touching you made it worse. I set you on the floor—I thought you were fainting."

In a move that seemed as natural as it should have been foreign to her, she reached for Larkin's hand before he retreated beyond her reach. His skin was calloused instead of soft, but as warm as the dog. He folded his fingers lightly around hers. Ava squeezed harder, wanting him to tighten his grasp. When he laced his fingers together with hers, anchoring her grip to his, she exhaled a sigh of relief, and inhaled the strength and comfort that seemed to flow through her with each hand.

"You whistled for Maxie?"

He answered with a sharp nod. But the thumb stroking the back of her hand was infinitely gentle. "I didn't know what else to do, except to make sure you didn't hit your head, and let the dog do what she does best."

Ava rubbed her cheek against Maxie's neck. "For a split second, when you were behind me—I think that's the warmest I've been in two years."

"I wanted to hold you," he confessed, the stroke of his thumb stilling against the pucker of scar tissue on her hand. "But I didn't want to make it worse."

"I'm okay," she reassured him, knowing that, for now at any rate, it was the truth. "I guess it's going to be a rough day. Usually, I don't have my attacks this close together. I'm to the point where I'll go days, weeks, without one."

"And then Larkin Bonecrusher stumbles into your life and sets your recovery back."

Ava continued to hug Maxie, although her gaze was focused on the self-recrimination in Larkin's expression. "You have nothing to do with what happened to me two years ago. I think you're moving my recovery forward, forcing me to deal with some things." She dropped her gaze to the link of their hands. "This is the second time I've reached for you today. And I'm not afraid." She forced her lips into the semblance of a smile when she realized the truth. "I'm also not counting."

"I am." There was that wry laugh that was husky and deep-pitched and so uniquely male. "Forty-four seconds. I figure those extra forty-one seconds are a gift. Or else you're still in the throes of the attack and don't know what's going on yet."

She squeezed his hand. "I know what's going on." When she didn't immediately protest, he pulled her hand to his lips and brushed a kiss over her knuckles. His beard tickled her skin, and she felt his warmth skitter along her arm and waken things inside her that had been frozen for two years. The pleasurable sensation more than the kiss itself surprised her. But the moment she straightened her fingers to study the sensitive spot, Larkin released her. She hastened to reassure him that it wasn't his touch that had startled her, but the fact she had enjoyed it. "Maybe there is some crossover between fiction and reality that makes me feel like I know you, that I'm safe with you—that…we're meant to be a team."

"I find myself thinking that, too," he admitted.

"I feel like I know you better than I should for someone I met just twenty-four hours ago. You are every bit the warrior I am, though in a different way. Maybe reading your books gives me insight into your soul, into the way you think."

Exactly. Only, he'd never written a book that she'd read. How could she be feeling such a strong connection to him? How could she feel like she knew everything about him that mattered? Shared values. Similar histories that offered them a unique understanding of each other. This crazy physical awareness of him.

But twenty-four hours?

Before the kidnapping she wouldn't have questioned her feelings for him. But perhaps she shouldn't be so ready to trust her instincts about this stranger. Helping him was one thing. Working beside him was also an acceptable decision. But falling for him?

With her mind firmly back in the present, Ava focused on the threat they'd been discussing before her panic attack.

"A little help?" When she curled her legs beneath her to stand, he tugged on her hand to pull her to her feet. She kissed Maxie's head before opening the treat jar on her desk and handing the dog a biscuit. "Good girl." The Great Pyrenees trotted over to the rug in front of the fireplace with her prize and Ava picked up the book that had fallen to the floor. "Here's what I wanted to show you." She opened the book to her publicity photo inside the back cover. "What do you think? Even if my alter ego has been leaked to the world, would any of my fans recognize me?"

Larkin studied the photograph of the woman she'd been before the scars and plastic surgery. "You're softer in this picture. Rounder cheeks, less tension beside your mouth. The suit clings to your curves. Your hair is all foo-fooey."

"Foo-fooey?" The stylist had curled and sprayed her hair within an inch of its life before that photo shoot.

Larkin closed the book in one hand and threaded the fingers of his other hand into the simple ponytail hanging over her shoulder. Although she held her breath, she didn't flinch as he sifted her hair through his fingers. "The Ava Wallace I know is a tomboy. Just as accomplished, just as creative, just as smart as this cosmopolitan A. L. Baines lady. Ava Wallace is in fighting shape. She's more streamlined. More practical. She has a sense of humor. She's more approachable to an average Joe like me."

Assuming he meant what he said, the praise made her self-conscious. Especially since she didn't think there was anything *average* about him. She took the book and placed it back on the shelf, reminding him of the truth. "She also has marks all over her body that will never completely go away, and it's hard to prove she's not as weak and fragile as people treat her when she loses it like I have today."

"Having PTSD doesn't mean you're weak. Have you ever known anyone fighting cancer or learning how to use prosthetics after losing their legs to an IED? They're warriors who refuse to give up the fight. Ava Wallace is no different. She's just seen more of life than people should ever have to." With the tip of his forefinger, he brushed aside the tendrils she usually let fall over her damaged cheek. When he tucked the long strands behind her ear, he cupped the side of her jaw and neck, resting the pad of his thumb against her cheek, suffusing her skin with a gentle heat for all of three seconds before pulling away. "Those scars don't diminish her beauty one bit. They prove she's a survivor, and I admire her for it. I can relate to that."

She wondered about the scars she'd seen on his body. Ava hadn't for one second thought they'd diminished how masculine or appealing he was. If anything, they'd made her curious to know more about him. They'd made her ache with compassion for the pain he must have suffered, both physical and emotional, to earn those scars. She supposed what a person found attractive in others changed as their unique experiences changed them. Not that the scars themselves were a turn-on, but they were a part of him. She found *him* attractive. Could she believe he might feel the same way about her? "You give unusual compliments."

Captured between her thoughts and those silvery-green eyes, the air between them charged with a pulsing energy. The moment felt intimate, magnetic, like some unseen force was pulling her closer to him.

But Larkin was the one to blink and break the spell. He laughed as he took a step back. "Hey, if you want me to fill up your *pretty little head* with cutesy words, I can do that for you, too, *baby*."

Ava swatted the air. "Stop it. Brandon and I were best buds growing up. He isn't that bad."

"You knew who I was talking about, though, didn't you."

She squished her face into an apologetic frown. "I did." Two years ago, she would have swatted the man who was teasing her right on the arm. But somewhere inside she knew that this bantering back and forth was already a huge step forward from where she'd been before this real Bonecrusher had entered her life, and she was grateful. "He believes he's being good to me, taking care of me. And I won't fault him for that. But when he pushes his way into my life to the point of suffocation, I… I feel like I grew up and moved on, while he's stayed as old-school as my grandfather was. He refuses to understand that I need to be in control of my life as much as I can."

"Because you know what it's like to have that control taken from you."

Ava nodded. This man seemed to know her better than the man who'd known her almost her entire life. "Other than the obvious signs of an assault, I haven't told him about what happened to me. He doesn't ask about it, either. I think he still sees me as an innocent teenage girl he once kissed."

"It shouldn't matter that he doesn't know what happened to you in Chicago. I can't respect a man who won't take no for an answer. If you don't want to be crowded and you're not comfortable with the way he talks to you, you have the right to not put up with that."

"Are you feeling rested enough for a little hike?" While spending time with Larkin seemed like a therapeutic catharsis for her, she needed a break to process the emotional changes she was going through. "Exercise and fresh air help clear my head."

"Whatever you need." He followed her into the kitchen where she gathered supplies to take with them. "Hopefully, they'll clear mine, too." When the joke earned him a sympathetic look instead of a laugh, he rinsed off their lunch dishes and loaded them into the dishwasher, helping her prepare to leave. "I wouldn't mind retracing the path I took to get here. If I can track my path back to where

I got started, maybe I'll see something that will jog my memory."

After calling Maxie from her lookout post at the back door, Ava put a harness with saddlebags on the dog and packed some water and energy bars along with dog treats in the pockets. "Are you a skilled tracker?"

"I don't know."

Once Ava released her, Maxie bounded to the front door, dancing in anticipation of their outing. "Fortunately, the Queen Mother of the Dragons here is."

The amused smile that matched hers for a moment faded into his beard. "Ava, would you still feel safe with me if I carried my own gun again? With bullets this time? You can say no. I don't want you to be afraid of me."

She considered his request for a moment, then opened the door to the garage and unlocked the climate-controlled storage closet where she kept the gun safe. "I'm less afraid of you having a gun than I am of being blindfolded or locked in a dark room, deprived of my senses. That's probably why that message made me go ballistic and shut down this morning. I didn't see the threat coming. I was blindsided."

"And a few minutes ago? I was pressing too hard, wasn't I. I triggered a flashback with one of my questions."

"We were talking about why I was kidnapped.

The hooded man didn't kidnap A. L. Baines. All he needed was a victim. Someone weaker than him who he could control for a few days. Someone who'd be too afraid to fight back." He held the door while she typed in the security code on the safe's electronic lock. "He picked me."

"You did what you had to do to survive. You played his game. You got out of there alive. Detective Charles said not every victim has been so lucky." She opened the heavy steel door and pulled his Hellcat, holster and magazine of bullets from the pockets in the door where she'd secured them while he'd slept last night. "You were smart. Resourceful. You endured. That shows a hell of a lot of strength, not weakness, if you ask me."

"You do give the weirdest compliments. But they have meaning for me. Thank you."

"I don't waste time on words I don't…mean." At his hesitation, she turned to see him looking past her to the display of weaponry she stored inside. He let out a low whistle between his teeth. "You know how to use all these?"

She pointed out the small armory while he knelt to strap on his ankle holster. "That's Grandpa's hunting rifle. His service pistol from Vietnam. Part of gun safety around here was knowing how to use and clean the weapon, how to safely store it and respecting that it was created to kill, not be played with." She pulled out the decorated leather-and-metal sheath hanging behind the Winchester rifle. "This sword is a gift from my publisher. I've used it to research sword fighting, but don't display it for obvious reasons."

"Because of fans like me who might recognize it." He reverently pulled the blade from its sheath and held it up to study the inscription. "This is a reproduction of Larkin's Bane-Slayer. And you use the bow and arrows to research Willow's character?"

He returned the sword to its sheath, and she hung it back in its place. "Grandpa taught me to hunt with a bow and arrow. I competed in some archery competitions in the summers here. It's what I know best, so that's why it's Willow's weapon of choice." She pulled her own small Glock from another pocket and loosened her belt to strap the gun onto her waist. "I learned to use this and the shotgun after my kidnapping."

Not that either would have saved her from the blitz attack that had rendered her helpless. But the hooded man might have thought twice about singling her out for his sick game if he'd seen the weapons. She felt more confident about defending herself now than she had two years ago, not only with the guns, but with the self-defense classes she'd started as soon as she was physically able after her recovery.

"You could give a guy a complex if he saw how well-armed you are."

She watched him check, load and secure his

weapon with a second nature she envied. "Does it bother you?"

"It bothers me that you feel you need an arsenal like this. I wish the man who hurt you could see all this. I wish he could see how much you've done to help me. How brave you are to face the things that frighten you, and you still come back fighting. He'd think twice about coming after you now." Again, the unusual compliment rang like truth inside her and warmed her from the inside out. He stepped back as she closed and reset the lock on the gun safe, then relocked the storage closet door. "But am I afraid of you and all those weapons? No. Willow isn't just the woman Larkin loves. He values her as a comrade in arms. He's not intimidated by her abilities or the crown she's supposed to wear." He held the door back into the kitchen open for her. "Trust me, I get Larkin."

Ava smiled shyly as she moved past him. Larkin loved Willow in her books. He valued her as a friend, companion and would-be lover. But how did this Larkin feel about Ava Wallace? Why did it feel like the lines between fiction and reality were blurring? Like the relationship she'd written on the pages had come to life and already felt deep and familiar?

Why wasn't she more worried about how much of herself she had shared with this man she'd met only yesterday? Did he really understand her in a way that no man ever had? Was she falling in love with the hero from her books? Or was she foolishly setting herself up for a disaster that could break her heart, if not cost her her life?

Too many questions with no good answers. She was beginning to understand the uncertainty and frustration Larkin must be going through with his memory gaps. She needed to get outside and get out of her head. Ava reached for Maxie's leash. "Are you ready to head out?"

"Lead the way."

Chapter Nine

Larkin's quest to retrace his path ended at the base of a forty-foot embankment. Ultimately, he did need Maxie's tracking skills and Ava's familiarity with the area to follow the path he'd left through the woods. In some places, dusty footprints, snapped twigs and swaths of dirt through a carpet of pine needles indicated where he must have rolled or dragged his feet, cutting an erratic path from these rocks to the gravel drive leading to her cabin. But there were other places where it looked like he'd been cognizant enough to erase his footprints and make false trails, sure signs that he'd been in survival mode against the enemy who wanted him dead. Only, as they reached the natural stair steps of craggy granite ledges and skinny trees with exposed roots leading up to a metal guardrail at the very top, he saw almost no evidence of anyone pursuing him.

Why hadn't they chased him through the woods? Had they assumed he was dead? If the man responsible for putting a bullet through his head believed he'd succeeded, or lied to his superiors about completing the job, then why was Roy

Hauser in town looking for him? If Larkin was in charge of a task force to take down an enemy, he wouldn't have assumed anything. He'd want the body as proof that the threat had been neutralized—either as his prisoner or in a morgue. And when Ava had driven him to the hospital, it had become evident to someone that he wasn't dead.

Was someone at the hospital in his enemy's pocket? When he'd shown up in the ER at Pole Axe's clinic, had someone called the would-be killer and informed him he had survived the attempt on his life? He still questioned the drugs Dr. Russell had given him. Unless the nurse had incorrectly dosed him. Or had his injuries simply been so severe that he was lucky he'd made it to Ava's place before he'd gone down for the count and slept the grogginess out of his system? Logic told him there was more than one player involved in the threats against him. Once he'd disappeared from the clinic, the hunt for Larkin Bonecrusher—or someone the enemy knew as Luke—had begun anew.

Did they have other means of tracking him? He swung his gaze to the brunette who was having an animated conversation with her big white dog, who was eating up the attention. Ava was every bit the intriguing woman warrior Willow Storm was. Only, fiction couldn't match the warmth, humor and vulnerability of the real thing. Man, he had a bad case of wanting something he probably shouldn't. But there was no denying his physical and emotional response to all things Ava Wallace. There was also no denying the guilt he felt at thrusting her into the middle of all this, despite her claims that challenging her to get involved was therapeutic for her.

He watched her pour water into a collapsible bowl for Maxie to lap up to help the panting dog cool down. After losing the trail a couple of times and doubling back, they'd been hiking at a relatively steady pace for almost two hours, covering several miles through steep terrain and a thick forest. Although he sensed that Ava had slowed her pace for his benefit, he'd been able to keep up, despite the battering his body had taken the day before and his limping stride. He wasn't too proud, though, to give his bum leg and aching shoulder a break and do a few stretches to ease the kinks before finding a relatively flat rock at the base of the cliff to sit on.

He tipped his head up. "Is that where we're headed next?"

When they heard the whoosh of a car passing by on the road above them, Ava confirmed what Larkin already suspected. "That's the highway that circles around the mountain. We were on it last night when we stopped at the scenic overlook. Several miles closer to town than we are now. Do you think this is where you rolled off the edge of the cliff?"

Larkin's gaze settled on a suspiciously dark spot on the rock beside him and he felt his stomach clench with a remembered desperation. He knelt to measure the size of the mark, confirming that the remnants of the bloody handprint matched his own. "Yeah. This is where Option B happened."

When he pushed to his feet, the rocks and trees swayed in front of him. Then he felt a gentle hand at his elbow. Ava guided him back to the rock and put a bottle of water into his hand. "Sit. You're looking a little pale."

He didn't think it was the altitude or the exertion so much as the jumble of memories flashing through his brain with the fuzzy definition of seeing oncoming headlights through the rain at night. "They disabled my car."

"A black SUV?" Ava opened her own water bottle and sat beside him to take a few drinks. She didn't push him to remember everything, yet her questions seemed to help draw out pertinent information.

"Yeah. Company car." He downed nearly half his water in one swallow as he relived the dizzying sensation of whipping around a hairpin turn while his SUV continued to pick up speed. "No brakes. Why didn't I check the status of the vehicle? That's a routine security check."

"You were in a hurry to get away. Maybe there wasn't time," she suggested.

"Or someone I trusted told me it was okay to go."

"Not having any brakes explains why you re-acted so strongly when I took a curve too fast driving into town."

He nodded as the empty places inside his head tried to tell him what he'd forgotten. "They were driving the same make of vehicle. When that black SUV passed us yesterday—"

"You ducked." She watched him take another drink before asking, "Who are *they*?"

"The security team I work for," he answered au-tomatically. He nearly spit out his water when he realized what he'd remembered. "My own people were chasing me."

"Roy Hauser was driving a black SUV this morning."

"The guy who was looking for me?"

She nodded. "That must be who you work for. BDS." She glanced up along the rocks before facing him again. "I have a friend who told me BDS uses the Ridgerunner Lodge at the top of the mountain for guests. You said you woke up in a hotel room and went to work. Is there a way to find out if Bell Design had something going on at the lodge this week? If you were there?"

Several pieces of the puzzle were floating around in his head, but they weren't yet falling into place. "Why would BDS be after me if I'm part of their team?"

"Maybe they're trying to help you. Mr. Hauser said he was worried about you."

Put a bullet in his head and make this all go away.

Larkin rose to his feet and studied the precipice above them. "They're the ones trying to kill me." He moved toward the rock face. "It all happened up there. The attempt on my life... Whatever happened before that is why they tried to kill me." He flattened his hand briefly against his belly and the miniature data stick making its way through his system. *That* had happened before losing control of his SUV and Option B. He set down the bottle of water and gripped the nearest outcropping of rock. "I need to get up there. If that's the crime scene, something's bound to jog my memory."

Ava's fingers wound around his forearm, pulling him back. "You can't make that climb. Not with your shoulder and knee. If one of them gives out, you could fall. Besides, if somebody drives past while you're up there, you'd be a sitting duck. If the wrong person sees you, they'll report you to Sheriff Stout or to BDS."

"I don't want you taking that risk."

She was already shrugging out of her backpack and unbuttoning her blouse. "I've climbed rocks before. Steeper than this."

"Without rappelling gear or a helmet? Ava..."

She peeled off the long-sleeved shirt and revealed the fitted white tank top she wore underneath. He was at once stunned to see the pale lines of old scars striping her upper arms like hash marks and awed to see the revelation of her true shape. Those baggy clothes disguised a lot of lean, beautiful curves. Ava was athletic and slim, but unmistakably female. He shook off both the flare of anger at seeing she'd been tortured like that, and the smack of desire that flooded the territory behind his zipper with unmistakable interest.

"Talk to me, Bonecrusher. What am I looking for when I get up there?" Hell. She was already on the first ledge, studying the outcropping above her, looking for her next handhold.

She needed him to stop gawking and think like an MP. Like an investigator. She needed him to be her comrade in arms and help her, since she was the one on the front line of this sortie. "Look for anything that seems out of place. Debris from a car accident. Tire tracks or footprints. Anything that doesn't seem natural to the scene."

She pushed herself up to the next ledge, tested the solidness of a tree root and used it to pull herself up above the level of his head. "There's blood on the rocks here, too." She glanced down at him with a grim expression. "There's a gouge in the bark, as well. Long and narrow, about the size of my finger."

"A bullet strike?"

"That'd be my guess." She pulled her phone from the back pocket of her jeans and snapped a few pictures. She was halfway to the road when she knelt on a wider ledge. "Oh my gosh. How many times did they shoot at you?" Ava held out a casing for him to see. "There are two more up here. We need to get the bullet Dr. Russell took out of your shoulder and compare the caliber. Prove that they all came from the same gun."

"I wasn't counting. And hug the damn rocks." He warned her back from the edge. A fall from this distance wouldn't be fatal, but she could break a bone if she hit something the wrong way. And if he couldn't make that climb, he wasn't sure he'd be able to catch her and break her fall, or get her to the help she might need, either. "Pay attention to your climb. We can talk clues once you're safely back down here."

"Roger that." She took more pictures before tucking the phone and casing into the pockets of her jeans and climbing another few feet to the next outcropping. The rocks were eroded in such a way that there were plenty of places to step onto or grab hold of. But for a man who'd been in free fall, those same protrusions had been blunt objects that had bruised ribs and split skin and pounded his body with an unforgiving assault. He wondered if the ache in his shoulder had more to do with the memories of the pain he'd endured that were trying to surface, or with his fear that Ava would grab the wrong tree or lose her footing and suffer a similar fate.

"Be careful," he called to her as she reached the top. He squeezed his eyes shut at the vivid recollection of rolling off the edge of the road into oblivion. But he opened them again just as quickly. He wasn't sure what he'd do from this distance if she fell, but he wanted to be ready to do something. He hated that she was the one putting herself at risk for him. "Watch for traffic, too. Make sure you're safe."

"I'm good." She grabbed hold of the guardrail and swung her legs over the top. He heard her boots crunch against the gravel, then fall silent as she reached the asphalt.

He wished he could see more than the top of her head and the swish of that long ponytail as she whipped her head from side to side to inspect her surroundings. "What do you see?" he demanded.

Ava leaned back to shout down the mountain. "The cleanest stretch of highway ever."

"What do you mean?"

She turned and leaned over the guardrail so that she didn't have to shout. "Seriously. It's like a road crew has been through here and picked up every scrap of trash and swept the road."

"No skid marks?"

"No." He supposed that made sense. If his brake lines had been cut, there wouldn't be any signs of a sudden stop. "Wait a minute."

"Ava?" When she disappeared from sight, Larkin's stomach clenched with worry. At least two vehicles drove past while she was out of his sight. Hopefully, there was a place to conceal herself up there, and she'd hidden herself from view. When several minutes passed without seeing her again, he damned the pain in his leg and shoulder and climbed onto the first ledge.

"What are you doing?" She reappeared at the top of the cliff and waved him back to the relatively flat slope at the base of the cliff. "I'm on my way down."

He watched her shimmy down the rocks with the confidence of a mountain goat. And though she never uttered one *ouch*, or showed any sign of distress, Larkin couldn't wait for her to be safely on level ground beside him again. When her boots hit the bottom ledge, he reached up to grab her by either side of her waist and lifted her down the last few feet. With her bottom tucked against the vee of his thighs and hips, he pulled her right up against his chest. He circled one arm around her shoulders and the other around her waist, and buried his nose in the fresh, herbal scent of her hair. He treasured the feel of her pressed against him and breathed her in—one, two, three.

He reluctantly loosened his hold, though he didn't push her away. "Why is it scarier to watch you do something dangerous than for me to do it myself?"

Her cheeks were flushed, and she was slightly breathless when she turned to face him, although whether her reaction was from the exertion of her climb or the momentary embrace, he couldn't tell. At least she wasn't lecturing him about this growing need to touch her. Then again, maybe she was just excited about whatever she'd discovered that she was eager to share. "I didn't see anything on this side of the highway." She pulled out her phone and brought up the pictures she'd taken. "There were tire tracks on the far side of the road. The grass in the ditch had been weed-whacked, but only a section of it. The highway department would have mowed everything along the shoulder. If you look closer, you can see the bottom of the stalks have been crushed."

"Like something heavy plowed through the ditch."

She nodded. "And then I saw this."

Ava swiped to a photo of a light-colored patch of unweathered rock that had been gouged out of the granite on the far side of the ditch. He spotted what she must have. "Something hit those rocks pretty hard."

"Like an out of control SUV?"

"They tapped my bumper and I spun out. I glanced off the rocks and flipped the SUV. Came to a stop on this side of the road." He remembered smacking his head against the window, then tumbling and tumbling. "They dragged me to the edge of the road."

"*They?* There was more than one man who attacked you?"

He squeezed his eyes shut, fighting to remember. There were no faces, only words.

It's not on him.

Grab his ID. I don't want anyone to link the body to us.

Nothing personal, Captain. Orders are orders.

Then the bullets and the falling.

Soft fingers brushed against his forearm. "Luke?"

His eyes snapped open. "Yeah. I'm okay." A big, furry weight leaned against his thigh, and he suddenly understood the power of Maxie's healing touch. He gazed down into Ava's deep blue eyes even as he scrubbed his fingers around Maxie's ears. "You called me Luke."

"I called you Larkin first. You didn't answer." She reached over to pet the dog, too. "You went away from us."

"I was remembering yesterday morning. Parts of it. I'm Luke..." Even without the initials on his key chain or any ID, the name finally fell into place. His chest expanded in a deep, unfettered breath as clarity returned. "I'm Luke Broughton. I remember!"

He barely heard her startled gasp as he picked her up and swung her around, celebrating the breakthrough he'd been half-afraid was never going to happen.

"I'm Luke Broughton. I remember now. Lucas Howard Broughton, Captain, United States Marine Corps, Retired. Honorable discharge due to chronic injury. Howard was my dad's name. I'm Luke…" He stopped when he realized he was staring straight into those cobalt eyes. A gust of warm breath whispered across his cheek as he assessed every inch of body contact between them. Although Ava's left hand was braced against his chest, their hips were cinched tightly enough to feel where hard lines ended and soft curves began. He'd latched on to one of those enticing curves with a possessive grasp of her bottom. Her other hand was still anchored at the back of his neck as he slowly set her on her feet. He held his hands out to either side of her, praying that what had felt so natural for him hadn't felt like confinement to her. "I'm sorry. I forgot the three-second rule."

"It's okay. Recognizing your name again is something worth celebrating." She pulled her hand from behind his neck, stroking it across his beard as she retreated. He looked for signs of panic or fear, but her eyes were following the path of her fingertips through the short hair of his beard. He saw curiosity. No, interest. No. Desire.

She touched a finger to the curve of his lip, but quickly pulled away as if she'd felt that same jolt of electricity arcing between them that he did. Damn, he wanted to kiss her. "Ava..."

She reached out to Maxie, and he grudgingly let the dog offer the grounding comfort she didn't want from him. "What about the men who tried to kill you?"

Luke shook his head. "I don't have faces yet. And I don't know the why." He patted his stomach. "Except they were looking for this. But I've got no clue what's on it."

"Let's focus on what we do know." She polished off her bottle of water and packed supplies back in Maxie's saddlebags, perhaps giving him time to cool his jets so another embrace like that wouldn't happen again. "You're Luke Broughton. We could look you up online or check military databases. Maybe I could ask Detective Charles to run a background check—if you were in military law enforcement, there's probably some sort of interagency cooperation he can tap into."

"Let's hold off on that. If the person who's after me is the one who hacked into Charles's computer, then a search like that would put him on alert. I don't want them to connect you to me in any other way beyond giving me a ride to the hospital yesterday."

"All right. What else do we know?"

"The chief of security at Bell Design Systems is looking for me. My car was sabotaged and run off the road where someone shot me."

"And to save yourself, you dove over the edge of a cliff and showed up on my doorstep." She pointed to the top of the cliff. "To hide their tracks, someone cleaned up where the accident ended. But they didn't do as good a job cleaning up where it began."

He handed her his water bottle to stow away so that they wouldn't leave any trash or trail. "If I only had the vehicle to match these tire treads to. I could trace the VIN back to BDS...or to Luke Broughton if I'm the owner. I'd be able to get an address at least."

"Want to bet the SUV that was destroyed in Scott Harold's junkyard was the one you were driving?"

He wouldn't take that bet. "Someone went to a lot of effort to clean up any evidence of the crime. Either I'm a big threat to BDS or I did something really bad."

"If my instincts aren't as rusty as I think they are, I'd vote for being a big threat. I'm the one who insisted on getting involved with this. You tried to walk away when you found out about my... history. You've gone out of your way to help me, not hurt me."

"I won't let anyone hurt you, Ava. Not even me," he promised.

She studied him for a moment, then nodded. "I believe you."

Nothing humbling about that. Man, he wanted

to be worthy of this woman. He wanted to be her partner, her protector. He wanted to see where a future with her might lead. But first, he had to resolve his past.

"So, we'll assume I'm a good guy. Even if my tactics don't always make that apparent." Although there were still some key gaps in his memory, enough of it was coming back that he remembered how to piece together clues and solve a crime. "I'd like to get that bullet Doc Russell took out of my shoulder and turn it and the casings you collected over to the authorities. Would you be offended if I said I want to give them to the state police and not your buddy Sheriff Stout?"

Her lips curled into a wry half smile. "I get it. Brandon thinks you intend to hurt me or use me, so he wouldn't be very sympathetic." She picked up her discarded blouse and shook off the dirt and pine needles that stuck to the cotton. "In the meantime, you and that secret information in your stomach are the only evidence that BDS or some individual at BDS has left to get rid of." She slipped it on and rolled up the sleeves. "But evidence of what? Any ideas yet about what's on that flash drive you ate?"

"We won't know for a few hours yet. My memory is coming back in bits and pieces, so we're still at a disadvantage. Hopefully, the flash drive will tell us everything else we need to know." He picked up her backpack and held it out to her. "All the more reason to get away from the road and back into the seclusion of the forest for a while longer. You said you had an idea for an escape plan if we need one?"

She thanked him for the pack. "I can show you if you want. How are you holding up? There's a direct route back to the cabin if you need to get home."

"I've been following that beautiful backside of yours all afternoon. I'm not about to stop now."

Her cheeks turned that adorable shade of pink.

"Not the worst thing a man's ever said to me." He loved that she was clever enough to throw his teasing words back at him. She shrugged into her backpack. Even with all those curves and skin camouflaged, he couldn't look away. "Do you want me to call you Luke now? Or stick with Larkin?"

"As long as you keep talking to me, I'm good."

"So am I." Those were the words he needed to hear. Ava was okay. They—whatever *they* were— were okay. She picked up her walking stick and whistled for Maxie. She nodded toward his injured leg. "Come on, Limpy. I promise this will be an easier hike."

Chapter Ten

A half hour later, they turned away from the creek they'd been following. Although Ava had been true to her word about this being an easier hike, Luke was feeling how hard he'd been pushing himself today.

"Are we there yet?" he teased, pretending his hip and knee weren't throbbing with every step.

She wasn't fooled. "You're really limping now. We need to take a break." Ava pointed to the thick grove of statuesque pine trees. "Fortunately, we're here. The trees camouflage it from the path. But if you climb up onto that first ledge, you'll see it."

"See what?" He followed her off the trail, climbing the easy footholds in the rocks. Once they'd cleared the granite ledge, a shallow, wide-mouthed cave opened up at waist level ahead of them. Luke blew out a long, awestruck whistle behind her. "The fortress at Stormhaven."

Ava smiled and gave Maxie a boost up to reach the next platform of rock that formed the floor of the cave. "You really are a fan of the *Chronicles*."

Although it was only about a five-foot rise, the rock face was steeper here. But Ava had discovered the best roots and safest crevices to grab to climb up into the cave. Luke followed the same path. Maxie was already sniffing around, looking for any little critters she needed to chase out.

"Can you make it okay?" By the time she turned to offer him a hand, he was pulling himself up into the cave beside her. He reached up to touch the roof of the cave and measure the head clearance he had to have to remain standing before turning to take in the view over the tops of the trees. "I see your inspiration. Granite walls. Hidden entrance. A view of the entire kingdom."

She grinned and shook her head. "Or the Hoback River Basin between the Wyoming and Wind River mountain ranges."

"I see rocks and trees and a river when I look out there. You see the Dragon Lands and Larkin's village." He followed her to a dented metal trunk tucked away against the cave wall several feet from the opening. Although the rivets at every joint showed signs of rust, the padlock she slid a key into was shiny and new. He helped her drag it away from the rocks so that the lid would open fully. Inside, he saw a folded camp chair, two blankets in plastic bags, a stash of metal bottles he assumed were filled with water and a faded blue metal tackle box. "The larder is stocked, I see. You could hide out here overnight if you had to."

"If the weather isn't too cold," she agreed. "Grandpa helped me set this up when I was fifteen. He's the only other person who's ever been here."

"Not even Sheriff Touchy-Feely? You said you two were close growing up."

"Nope. Even Grandma never ventured out here. She said a teenager needed her privacy, and as along as Grandpa thought it was safe, she approved."

"I'm honored to make the short list of guests."

Ava pulled out the camp chair and he set it up. Meanwhile, she tossed one of the blankets out, which Maxie immediately scratched at before circling around several times and lying down on it. "I don't keep perishables here because of scavengers. Just some basic supplies in case I misjudge the length of a hike and need to rest, or I need a place to get away." More secluded than her cabin? This woman really did find security in being alone. Next, she opened up the tackle box to reveal her stash. "Flashlight and batteries. Matches. Pocketknife."

He pulled out a weathered journal and box of pencils. "Something to record your inspirations? Or a secret diary?"

Ava snatched it away and tucked it back inside the bottom of the tackle box.

Luke laughed. "Ah. Secret diary. The lovestruck ramblings of a teenage girl?"

She swatted his arm. "There are things in that journal that will never see the light of day. I do write out here sometimes. But I'll put my computer notebook in my backpack and enjoy the fresh air for a few hours." She gestured to the camp chair for Luke, then closed the trunk. "Have a seat. I'm afraid you're overdoing it."

"I'm fine. I'll take an energy bar and one of those bottles of water Maxie is carrying, though, if she'll share."

"Sure." Ava pulled her lips tight against her teeth and let out a shrill whistle. The Great Pyrenees immediately popped up and trotted over to her mistress.

"The dragon summoning that Willow uses. You've whistled for her before."

Ava pulled out snacks and a bottle of water for them both. "Not everything in my life is part of my books." She removed the saddlebags and gave the dog's back and flanks a vigorous petting before urging the dog to curl up on her blanket again. Then Ava sat on the corner of the trunk, and they all took a few minutes to relax and recoup their energy. "How did you become a Bonecrusher fan?"

"A buddy introduced me to the series on a deployment. When I was in the hospital at Landstuhl, I reread through every one of them. It was a distraction from the pain and the loss. And yeah, I fantasized about gettin' busy with Willow." He hoped the color warming her skin meant she was flattered by his subtle compliments. And yes, now that he'd put a face to the heroine, he'd fantasized about the real thing, too. He washed down a bite of the bar with a drink of water and leaned back in the nylon canvas seat to take in the mountain scenery. He understood how this place could feel like a haven, isolated in some of the most gorgeous country he'd ever seen. "Mostly I related to that sense of having a quest, a mission to fulfill. There was a purpose to what your characters were doing. Just like the Corps. Just like my efforts to heal and make it through rehab. And the team in your books, the bonds they share, it felt like my unit. We weren't dealing with sorcerers and hundred-year-old curses, but the feeling was the same. Hell, I miss those guys." He stuffed the last of the bar into his mouth and took another drink. "So, what's stopping you from finishing the next *Chronicle*? Speaking strictly as a fan, you kind of left us hangin'."

"You, too, huh?" She dabbed at the crumbs clinging to her lips, and he silently warned that most interested part of his anatomy to keep things casual. "I think I took a left turn in the last book by introducing Lord Zeville, and I'm not sure how to come back from it." Nope. Putting her lips around the bottle for another drink wasn't helping his lower half remember to mind its manners. Luke had to shift to a more comfortable position and look away from the temptation. "Plus, there's the whole Larkin/Willow thing. I swear if those two don't get together, I'm going to lose half my readers. The other half can't get enough of the sexual tension, and fear it will go away if those two ever come out and say the three magic words, and—like you said—get busy. It would be such a big moment in the series. I don't know if I could get the details right."

"Are you kidding?" Did she not feel the sexual tension filling up this cave? Whether she believed it or not, the woman got every detail right, as far as he was concerned. "That make-out session in the dungeon in the last book was pretty hot. I was certain they were going to seal the deal then. If the rebels hadn't chosen that moment to rescue them…" Luke could have sworn his own skin was heating beneath his beard. "I have to tell you I got a lot of mileage from that scene. I finished it a dozen different ways in my imagination. That's vivid, compelling writing."

"Thanks." Her smile thanked him for the praise, but the stroke of her knuckles along her scarred cheek revealed the uncertainty within her. "I think because of what happened to me, I'm afraid to let go the way I'd need to in order to create that kind of closeness again. How am I supposed to get Larkin and Willow to kiss or touch, much less make love, when I can't even do it myself?"

"You let me touch you. For three seconds. For more than three seconds a little while ago." She laughed at the reminder, but it was a sad, self-deprecating sound.

He remembered something one of his doctors had said to him when he'd despaired about ever being whole enough to be useful to the Corps again. *"Turn your shortcomings into an advantage. If you can't be as physical as you once were, then be more mental."* Although he'd made a joke that being mental was the problem, the doctor hadn't laughed. *"Be smarter, Captain Broughton. Use your brains if your body fails you. A good investigator has to be smarter than the bad guy, not faster."*

Could that philosophy work for Ava, too? "Maybe you shouldn't try to be the same writer you were before your kidnapping. Embrace who you are now. Let those emotions work for you. You've changed. Maybe Willow needs to change, too."

Her blue eyes were dark like midnight in the shadows of the cave. But he knew she was searching his expression, considering his suggestion, wanting to believe it could work. "How do you mean? It's hard enough to talk about the kidnapping. I don't think I could write about it and share it with the world."

"You don't have to. But there are elements of your life now that could enrich a story you couldn't have told two years ago." He left the chair to kneel in front of her. He gently took her hand and clasped it between his. "One one-thousand. Two one-thousand. Three one-thousand." Then he released her and sat back. "Is that something you can work into your story? The three-second rule? Maybe Lord Zeville put a spell on Willow while he had her in his palace chambers, and now Larkin and Willow can only touch for three seconds before her skin burns—"

"Or she turns on him, thinks he's her enemy." Luke had only suggested the germ of an idea, but Ava was turning that idea into a whole story. "They'd have to break the spell by completing a quest."

He splayed his fingers on the flat of his stomach, reminding her of the flash drive. "Deciphering a mysterious text?"

"They'd have to find the text first." She snapped her fingers and stood. "That's brilliant. If they touch too long, it leaves another scar. It brands her."

"You sure you want to add scars to your story? Won't that dredge up—"

"Of course, he won't want to leave a mark on her, so he'll pull away. That push-pull or wanting, but denying it, that's sexual tension. I'll have to work out some kind of action scene where they're forced to hold on to each other, like dangling over the edge of a cliff. She'll turn on him, but he won't let go, no matter how hard she comes at him. The spell will backfire on Zeville. Larkin and Willow will be battling each other—"

"—with Larkin being careful not to actually hurt her because she's bewitched—"

"—and voilà! A pair of sword thrusts and Zeville is dispatched. Destroyed by the very war he tried to create." Ava was pacing circles around the cave, moving her hands in excited gestures, including imaginary sword fighting, as she thought out loud. She shimmered with a kind of creative energy that was as foreign to Luke as it was exciting to watch in her. She shooed Maxie off the blanket and quickly folded it up. "Are we done here? Is Stormhaven enough of a backup plan for you? You think you could find it on your own if you had to? It's not a very well-marked path."

"That's one of the things I like about it." He helped her repack the trunk. "Cabin to creek. Creek to trees. Stormhaven is tucked in behind them."

She locked the trunk and pocketed the key. "I can bring out more supplies tomorrow if you think we need them. Right now, I'd like to get to my computer. Get a couple of hours of writing in yet tonight."

He followed her down the incline and helped her guide Maxie safely down between them. "Is this how being a writer works? You get an inspiration, and you run to your computer?"

"Sometimes. There are days when the words flow out of my fingers and I can't get them down fast enough. And there are others when it's an uphill battle to get a single page written." She hooked Maxie to her leash and headed for the trees. "It's been a while since an idea has really spoken to me like this. I think you're on to something. I need to write who I am now. My characters will be more battle weary. They'll be choosier about who they trust. I have a feeling my voice will be a little grittier. But the ending of the story arc is darker, anyway. And when I reach the resolution and happily-ever-after, it will be a bigger emotional payoff. So, can we go?"

There was not one whit of hesitation to her demeanor now. Luke was pleased to see her so fired up about her work, and he was glad that, in some small way, he'd been able to help—both as a fan of the books, and as a fan of Ava Wallace. "We're good. Stormhaven will do for Option B. Let's get you home to work."

They hadn't yet reached the trees when Luke heard the humming overhead. The familiar buzzing sound was as relentless as a mosquito but reminded him of things far more dangerous. He shaded his eyes and tilted his face to the sky until he pinpointed the black, bug-shaped drone flying back and forth overhead, closer to the creek they'd followed here. Luke got an uneasy feeling in the pit of his stomach. He'd kill for a pair of binoculars right now, to either confirm or negate his suspicions.

He sensed rather than saw Ava move in beside

him, her face turned to the clouds, as well. "I saw one of those this morning. People use them to get spectacular video or pictures of the mountains. When they're up that high, there are no trees or rock formations to get in the way."

"That one doesn't belong to a tourist. It's flying in a search grid." He patted his hip, his instincts telling him to radio in the drone's position. Only, there was no radio. There was no team to call. There was only this precious woman and her dog. "Where was the drone you saw this morning?"

"About a mile north of here, higher up the mountain." Closer to where she'd scaled the cliff below the scene of his *accident*.

"This one's a lot closer." Ignoring the twinge in his shoulder, he spanned her waist and lifted her onto the lower ledge of Stormhaven. "Get back in the cave."

"I doubt they can see us through the tree cover."

"Do you want to take that chance?"

When her blue eyes met his, he silently let her know he wasn't risking their safety on the possibility he could be wrong.

Ava offered a quick nod of understanding and reached for the dog. "Maxie?"

He boosted the dog up. "If it's rigged with infrared, the surrounding rocks and chill of the cave should mask our heat signature."

"Infrared?" Her hand was there to help him over the lip of the opening. "I felt like I was being watched this morning. I thought I was just being me. Paranoid. You think they're searching for you?"

"They're searching for something."

"The forestry department uses drones."

"All right. I won't rule out that it has a benign purpose. But I'm not gambling our lives on it." Luke stood as close to the opening as he dared. Definitely a search grid. The drone had moved half a klick to the south and resumed its linear flight pattern. "BDS has equipment like that."

She tugged him back from the opening of the cave when the relentless drone buzzed toward their position. "Bell Design Systems? How do you know?"

He was glad to see her keeping hold of Maxie's leash. If an infrared-armed drone could pick up something as small as a fox or pika on its scope, it could certainly pick up the dragon queen loping through the woods. "We used one like it for aerial surveillance outside Kandahar." He watched the drone easily from this vantage point, but if the search grid shifted in this direction, they'd be moving deeper into the cave. "My buddy V was obsessed with the things. He was always tinkering with them, extending their range, adding a stronger zoom feature to the lens, more sensitive radar."

"Who's V?" Ava asked.

"Ryan Voltaggio. We came up through MP training together. Our unit…" He glanced over the jut of his shoulder at her, realizing what she'd just done. "I know Ryan Voltaggio."

She squeezed his arm and smiled at yet another breakthrough. "It may be a long shot. But can you call the Marine Corps and ask for his phone number? Maybe he's the friend you remember calling."

The fist of another memory squeezed his heart and he shook his head. "V never made it home."

"Oh, Luke. I'm so sorry." Her fingertips grazed his forearm again. A sympathetic touch.

A touch he needed like his next breath. Luke swore at the pain ripping through him and pulled her into his chest. He wound his arms around her, backpack and all. Her walking stick clattered on the stones at their feet and her arms snuck around his waist. He squeezed his eyes shut against the violent, bloody images bombarding him. The initial flash of an explosion. The helplessness at seeing his men so close to the blast. The betrayal. The loss. The searing pain.

He buried his face against the juncture of her neck and shoulder, breathing in her clean, natural scent. Catching the long strands of silky hair in his beard, tangling the two of them together. He clung to her warmth. Her strength. The mental toughness that was far stronger than his own at the moment.

He locked her in his arms and they rocked together as the nightmarish memories buffeted him. He held on, and she held him right back, well past any three-second mark. "I'm so sorry," she whispered against his ear. "He was your friend."

"Of all the things to remember." He palmed the back of her head, sifting his fingers through her ponytail, needing the reality of thick, soft waves filling his palm. "I lost four people on my team that day. Plus, this kid we knew. We'd taken him under our wing, gotten close to him. He was our friend. At least, we thought he was. It all happened so fast. There wasn't time to save anybody. They were all just…gone."

Her arms tightened around his waist. Her fingers fisted in the back of his shirt. "Is that when you got hurt? I saw the scars." She turned her lips against his ear and nuzzled his neck. "I'm so sorry."

Yes. This was what he needed. Warmth. Reality. Ava.

He brought his other hand up to brush the loose tendrils off her cheek. He cupped her jaw between his hands and tilted her face up to his. Her blue eyes were shiny with unshed tears. She felt pain for *him*. She already had so much pain of her own. He caught the first tear with the pad of his thumb when it spilled onto her cheek.

And then he realized it was his own tear that had dropped onto her skin.

"Luke…" Her lips parted, trembled, and Luke dipped his mouth to capture hers. Soft. Full. Still.

He heard her quiet gasp and a moment of sanity returned.

"Oh, God." What was he doing? He lifted his head, but he wasn't a strong enough man to release her entirely. His fingers shook with the effort to pull them from her warm skin. Her eyes were dark with emotion, but he couldn't read them. Ah, hell. He'd probably scared her. "I'm sorry. I overstepped a lot of boundaries. Is it okay if I kiss—"

Ava pushed up onto her toes and sealed her lips to his.

Luke rocked back on his feet as she leaned into him. He might be the startled one this time, but he made a quick recovery. He braced his body to take her weight and tunneled his fingers into her hair to cup the back of her head. He supped at her mouth, discovering every soft pillow, every agile corner—and then he sampled them all again, drinking in her shy forays and welcoming responses. The feel of Ava's hidden curves flattened against him; the gentle dance of their tongues, and her growing eagerness to touch and taste him, kindled a heat inside Luke that flowed through his veins into every part of him, chasing away the nightmares and grief, filling him with strength and hope and the most perfect sense of rightness he could remember either before or after the amnesia.

Ava skimmed her palms across his beard, smiling against his mouth at what must be a ticklish sensation. Then she slipped her arms around his neck, sliding her hand against his hair, hugging him close. His hands bumped into the backpack she still wore, but it was little deterrent to him finding more of her body to touch, more heat to absorb. His palm wound up on the sweet curve of her bottom. He squeezed her through her jeans and lifted her into his aching response to her healing kiss. Her arms tightened around his neck, holding on as her feet left the cave floor. Her legs parted naturally, falling around his hips and thighs as they traded kiss after kiss. The tips of her breasts beaded and poked him through the layers of cotton between them. So responsive, so proud, so perfect.

He heard a breathless whimper in her throat. Her clutching hands and generous kiss fueled his own groan of frustration. He heard the rasp of denim against denim, and the lazy yawn of the dog stretched out beside them. Maxie's indifference to the embrace was as good as a vote of approval, and Luke's breath gusted against Ava's throat at his sigh of satisfaction while he nibbled on the warm beat of her pulse there.

What he didn't hear was the hum of the drone.

Awareness of another kind washed over him like the splash of a cold mountain stream. Luke ended the kiss, hugging Ava lightly in his arms and turning slightly so that he was between her and the entrance to the cave. He scanned the sky above them and beyond the trees. Either the machine had run out of juice, or whoever was flying it had moved on to a new search grid. "We're alone again. They moved their search elsewhere."

"It's gone? We're safe?" He nodded before resting his chin at the crown of her hair. He took in a deep lungful of air to steady his breathing and regain his senses. Her arms retreated to his waist and he felt her fingers press into the small of his back. "Are you all right now?" she whispered against his collar.

"I haven't been this right since… I don't think anything's ever felt this right," he admitted, then tightened his arms around her, backpack and all, and buried his nose in the intoxicating scent of her hair. "God, woman. You turn me inside out. Especially since I know how uncomfortable you are with intimacy."

"I'm not completely uncomfortable with it. I just need to be in control of it."

He eased his hold on her, not wanting to push his luck. "It sounds naughty, but control me all you want. Any way you need to. Yell at me. Push me away. Sic the dragon on me if I go too far."

"I can't do that. Maxie likes you." She straightened the blouse that had ridden up between their bodies and his roaming hands. "Besides, I'm healing, remember? That was pretty good therapy for me."

He laughed. "It was damn good therapy for me. I'm sorry I dumped on you. The memory of that suicide bomb kind of blindsided me when it all came back to me."

"I know the feeling. I like the way you handle it better. I'll have to remember that next time I have a panic attack—kiss, don't collapse." She reached up and stroked her fingers through his beard again, reawakening all the nerve endings that were just starting to chill. If she was this fascinated with touching a few days' worth of stubble, he was never shaving again. "This tickles when I kiss you. It's...stimulating." She abruptly pulled away as if she was feeling the electricity reigniting between them, too. "I'm attracted to you, Luke. I feel a connection to you. That wasn't just about offering comfort. I wanted to kiss you. I liked...kissing you. I can't remember the last time my blood pumped that hard for any good reason. You needed me, and I wanted to be there for you. It felt freeing. Normal. What normal people do, I mean. Not that you're not normal." Her cheeks turned that healthy shade of pink. "I'm not saying this right. I'm out of practice with any kind of relationship—"

He pressed his thumb to her lips to hush her protests. "I liked kissing you, too. And I intend to do it again. Often, if you let me." He brushed her hair off her face and tucked it behind her ear before leaning in and pressing a gentle kiss right against the scar on her cheek, in case she had any doubts that he wanted to taste every last inch of her. When she was ready. "But we're still not going to rush anything. I'd never forgive myself if I scared you back into your shell. And then there's that whole bad guys trying to kill me thing I should probably take care of." He stepped back, putting an arm's length of distance between them before holding out his hand. "Compromise?"

"You and your Option B. Always got to have a backup plan." She reached out and took his hand. "I can do that."

He checked the sky once more, giving an all clear before climbing down out of the cave. He captured her hand again as soon as all three of them were on ground level, heading back to the cabin. They were well beyond the count of three and still holding hands when he spoke again. "If you trust me in your kitchen, I'll cook dinner so you can write. I can't wait to read the next Bone-crusher book."

She squeezed his hand, assuring him she was okay with the ongoing link between them. It wasn't a sexy come-on or a promise of forever. But to Luke, her ability to trust him with holding her hand meant as much as the smile she gave him. "You know, for the first time in a long time—I can't wait to write it."

Chapter Eleven

Luke should have asked for pajamas when Ava had bought him supplies in town. His new jeans were still a little stiff and itchy, and he really wanted to take off his T-shirt and bandage to let the stitches in his shoulder get some air and dry out after his shower. On his own, he'd sleep in his briefs or nothing at all. But he could hardly prowl around Ava's cabin in the middle of the night in his underwear or his birthday suit. Especially since she was up equally late on the sofa across the living room at the tail end of a marathon writing session that had started almost as soon as they got home from Stormhaven, and resumed right after the grilled burgers and veggies he'd made for dinner.

The cabin was locked up tight, but he'd been cautious about leaving on too many lights that might draw the attention of anyone flying a drone overhead, searching for them. The single lamp he had on at Ava's desk where she'd set him up to work on her computer provided the only illumination in the entire house, save for the light reflecting off their respective computer screens and the patches of moonlight sneaking in through drawn window shades and curtains. After cleaning up the flash drive that had finally made its appearance, and reading the contents, he had no doubt an enemy was still searching for him to complete the task of silencing the veteran Marine who'd blown the whistle on BDS's illegal activities—and the brave woman who had deigned to help him because she needed to be needed, and she wanted to disprove her misguided belief that she was weak or useless.

Not for the first time that night, Luke turned in his chair to glance over at Ava, his dark-haired warrior, to see with his own eyes that she was safe, that he hadn't done anything else to jeopardize her safety despite her willing cooperation with his investigation.

And not for the first time that night, Luke let his gaze linger on the woman who had grown to mean so much to him in such a short time. Who needed a slinky peignoir when that well-worn pair of running shorts hugged her sweet derriere and showed off those long, fit legs as she sat on the couch with her toes tucked beneath a sleeping Maxie? Even the oversize man's T-shirt she wore for a top only served to point out the wonderful differences between a man's blockier shape and the swells and dips that made a woman's figure so irresistibly interesting. Bopping her head to whatever tune was playing inside the noise-canceling headphones she wore, she stared at the screen while her fingers flew over the keyboard as if possessed.

The pillow beneath her laptop couldn't completely mask the faded scars that dotted her thighs and disappeared beneath the hem of her shorts, matching the similar trail he'd seen on her arms earlier. While the marks of torture didn't take one thing away from his body's physical response to her, the visible evidence of some bastard hurting her triggered a primitive, protective anger in him. As strong as Ava was, as much as she wanted to fight her own battles, if there was breath in his body, no one would ever hurt her again.

Perhaps sensing the intensity of his thoughts, Ava looked up from her work to meet his gaze. Although she raised an eyebrow, silently asking if anything was wrong or if he'd found out something new, Luke smiled and waved aside her query. He wasn't sure exactly how the creative process worked, but he was quickly learning that too many interruptions messed with the flow of getting the words down on the page. He'd get an impatient huff followed by a polite smile, which were infinitely worse than a pointed lecture or one of her sarcastic comebacks.

He'd already asked her to stop for dinner and to show her the information in the files he'd taken from BDS—evidence of illegal transactions and moving money around to hide payments into an account marked "JR" from overseas investors for technology BDS was designing for the American military. Ava had asked some smart questions that helped him recall what had put him onto the discrepancies in company records in the first place. And her suggestion that he give himself another night's sleep to allow his battered brain a chance to completely heal and recover other pertinent information, such as what he had done with the evidence on the flash drive *before* the car chase and bullets, if anything—and where he'd been heading when his SUV had spun out of control—made good sense. Although he suspected continuing that conversation would gradually draw out the information he needed, he'd already turned her life upside down this weekend. He wasn't going to let his presence here impact her work, especially now when she claimed to be having some sort of breakthrough. With a sweet little wink, her head resumed its bobbing to the music, and she turned her attention back to the keyboard.

Luke spun back to his own workspace, looking beyond the holstered gun he was keeping within easy reach on the desk beside him to the tiny clock in the corner of the computer screen—1:15 a.m. He wondered how late she'd stay up writing. He wondered if she could understand his need to keep her in his sight, both for her security and for the grounding sense of calm that being with her these past two days had given him. He might not know who his enemies were in the world outside this cabin, but here with Ava he knew peace and trust and—like she'd said up at the cave he'd dubbed Stormhaven—normalcy. He could live this life. Spending time in the outdoors with a great dog, watching Ava write—helping her brainstorm an idea or two. He'd need a job, of course, so he could stay out of her hair while she created her fantasy world on the computer, but he could come home to a brilliant, brave woman and greet her with another one of those kisses that damn near made his body explode. He liked the way she thought. He admired her talent. He appreciated her strength. As inevitably as Larkin Bonecrusher and Willow Storm were destined to be together, he was falling in love with Ava Wallace.

With that sobering thought, he pulled up the internet and focused on his own work, researching the players at Bell Design Systems, wondering which of them—or if all of them—wanted him dead.

The reason why BDS had put a hit on him was obvious. Some very powerful people were doing some very illegal things. Selling plans for US military tech to a subversive Chinese faction was a threat to national security. Maybe the insurgents intended to build the tech and start a revolution in their own part of the world, or maybe they were paying to have the inside scoop on what America and her allies might be using in a war zone or on border patrol duty.

Either way, this sort of industrial espionage and infiltration had been part of what he'd been up against when he'd been promoted to investigative duties as an MP. He'd recognized the money laundering in accounts and the encrypted emails that included both schematics and negotiations. Although he suspected these files didn't tell the whole story, along with his testimony, they would certainly give a federal prosecutor, or even the IRS, plenty of material to obtain a search warrant to go through all of BDS's files to find more evidence and pinpoint all the players involved in the illegal transactions. If he'd been as smart as he thought he was, he'd made more than one copy of the files and had hidden them somewhere, or he had sent the originals on to someone else. But maybe the perp at BDS had blocked his messages or rerouted his voice mails. Maybe that's what had led to the desperate act of fleeing from the people he worked for and swallowing the flash drive. He'd be a fool to risk his life for one little data stick, knowing that destroying it and killing him would eliminate the threat to BDS. He must have had a backup plan in mind that he'd forgotten, a contact he'd been trying to reach in case things went south for him.

They had gone way south, and he still had no idea who he was up against, and how much anyone in the outside world knew about the secrets he'd uncovered.

Take a deep breath. Do your job. You got this.

Luke pulled up a recent magazine interview and stared into the eyes of the main man himself—Gregory Bell. The founder and CEO of Bell Design Systems was a brilliant engineer in his own right. More than that, he was an adept businessman who'd built BDS from the ground up. Bell knew how to hire the right people, and when to buy out the competition or sell off a division, to turn his company into a billion-dollar empire. So why would a guy like that resort to under-the-table dealings? Was someone else in his company dealing with the Chinese faction? Or did the white-haired man in the tailored suit have a secret to hide? Blackmail to pay? A lover he was keeping in diamonds and a penthouse? Good old-fashioned greed? Did he have a personal vendetta against someone that made him willing to risk the expensive contracts he had with the government and military? The article included a picture of Bell with his wife and three daughters. But while the information sounded familiar because of his job, any spark of recognition about the CEO himself did not.

The next player he pulled up was Roy Hauser, the chief of security. Hauser had hired him earlier this year, fresh after his Marine Corps discharge, to work as a military consultant and do background research on potential hires, and to help provide security for BDS executives and visiting guests, including the Chinese dignitaries he remembered from the hotel at the top of the mountain. What had Ava called it? Ridgerunner Lodge. He'd mistakenly thought he'd uncovered some hacking activities from their guests or from someone in IT who'd been working with them. There'd been a late-night meeting with Hauser where he presented his suspicions about someone in the company leaking information to the Chinese.

The next morning he'd been racing down the mountain highway in a car with no brakes and a contingency of BDS security hot on his trail.

He had no idea how many people at BDS were involved in the treasonous business activities. He had no idea if Hauser or Bell were involved, or if Hauser had reported Luke's findings and had inadvertently alerted the wrong person in the company. The men pursuing him could simply be taking orders. Whoever was behind this had probably labeled Luke as the traitor so that they could use him as a scapegoat, eliminate him and his evidence and go on their merry way, making illegal millions and endangering his fellow military men and women.

He had to have told someone outside of BDS what he'd found. Or at least been on his way to do so. But who? Who would he have trusted enough to share the secret with? A military contact? An attorney? State police? The FBI? He'd told Ava he'd called a friend in the Corps the day before all this started. Was that the connection he'd shared his suspicions with?

He needed to make phone calls.

He needed to find numbers first. They'd probably been programmed into the phone that was taken from him. BDS had that, too. They could know his contacts before he did.

Step one was to recapture those last elusive bits of his memory. Who did he think was responsible for these crimes? Who would he have called for backup?

Then he heard a soft snore from behind him and smiled.

Who would he call besides his very own Willow Storm?

Time to give his battered brain a break. With the clock ticking past two in the morning, Luke strapped the Hellcat around his ankle and powered down the computer. It was nice to be able to stuff the data stick into his pocket instead of feeling the need to hide it down his gullet again.

Now that Ava was clearly ready to turn in, Luke got up and went to the sofa. When Maxie sat up in curiosity, he put a finger to his lips, as though the dog would understand the warning not to wake up her mistress.

Ava's lashes were long and dark against her pale skin, and they barely fluttered as he saved the story on her laptop and removed the headphones.

When she didn't stir, Luke stretched his shoulder to test its tenderness and strength. Confident that he was the man for this job, he slipped his arms beneath Ava's knees and back and picked her up, laptop and all. He held her for a few seconds, waiting to see if she'd wake or panic at being confined to his arms. But when she snuggled her cheek against his chest with a sleepy sigh, he turned toward the stairs.

"Come on, girl," he whispered to Maxie, and the dog followed as he carried Ava upstairs to her bedroom and laid her on the bed.

He pulled the sheet and quilt over her and set the laptop on the bedside table. But when he spotted his name on the middle of the screen, he picked up the laptop and read the page she'd written there. The voice of the A. L. Baines he knew leaped off the page and he scrolled back to the beginning of the scene.

Although the chapter took place between Larkin and Willow in a cave where they'd been stranded after a rescue from Lord Zeville's castle, he found at least two instances where she'd slipped and typed in his name instead of Larkin's. Luke stood there beside the bed in the shadows, completely engaged in the newest chapter of the *Chronicles*. Son of a gun. It turned into a love scene. Luke felt a punch of desire in his gut. It wasn't a technical love scene with a bunch of bells and whistles. It was a tender, slow and sensual, okay, a freakin' hot love scene between Larkin and Willow.

A drowsy voice interrupted him before he reached the last paragraph. "Nosy. You better not plagiarize my book or leak that onto the internet."

Luke sank onto the edge of the bed beside her. "Is this what you want to have happen between us?"

Her eyes opened wide. "What?"

"You used my name a couple of times. Slip of the imagination?" he teased.

Suddenly wide awake, Ava sat up and snatched the computer off his lap. She closed the program and shut the laptop completely, stuffing it under the pillow next to her. "That's a rough draft. Not even my editor gets to read that version. I spew out all my ideas, and then I go back and make it pretty."

"It gets better than that?" He didn't have a creative bone in his body, and her talent was oozing out her pores. "Don't tell me you can't write a love scene. That was…really good."

"It's fiction."

Fortunately, Luke Broughton had other talents. "It doesn't have to be."

And there was that beautiful blush he loved. "How did I get upstairs?" Unexpectedly shy about a man sitting on her bed flirting with her, or maybe realizing too late that she'd been vulnerable to him while she'd dozed, she pulled the covers up and hugged them to her chest. "What about your shoulder?"

"Loved every second of carrying you."

"You know what I mean. Did I hurt you?"

"I loved having you in my arms. Figured if you were sleeping, I didn't have to count." Her hair hung loose and wavy around her face and shoulders. Luke brushed the long waves back behind her ear, wanting to let her know there was nothing she needed to hide from him. "You're a snuggler, by the way, when you lower your guard. I loved every second of that, too."

She briefly turned her cheek into his palm before scooting away and changing the subject. "Did you find out everything you needed from the data stick? Is BDS selling their tech to someone besides our military?"

He nodded, knowing he shouldn't push her to admit she wanted the same thing he did. That love scene could have been an extension of her subconscious mind, not a conscious wish. And he wanted her fully with him when he made love to her, whether it was an hour from now or a year from now. Providing, of course, he survived this mess at all. "I still don't know who the players are. But I uncovered something big. When I alerted Hauser to what I found, I set a chain of events in motion."

"You think he's behind the attempt on your life? Did he shoot you?"

"I don't know." With his mind focused back on where it needed to be, Luke got up, allowing her to slide farther under the covers. "I do know that as long as I'm alive and the information I found can destroy BDS, someone will be coming after me. I hope I called for backup before everything went FUBAR. That someone I trust is out there looking for me."

"I hope so, too."

"I'd better let you get your sleep. Looks like you're mentally all played out."

"Thanks for the inspiration."

So that chapter *was* about the two of them. At least, a little bit.

"Anytime." He patted the bed, urging the dog to jump up and curl up beside her. "Maximillia Madrona Draconella Reine will keep you safe tonight."

"Good night, Larkin."

"Good night, Willow."

Chapter Twelve

Luke woke to the sound of muffled screams. What the hell?

He rolled over in bed, orienting himself to the darkness. Not screams, but whimpering, muffled words that didn't make sense. He glanced over at the clock on the table beside him—4 a.m. Then he heard a thump, panting. A big dog scratching at a door.

Luke swung his legs over the side of the bed. Although the doors were closed between them, he recognized the sounds from the morning before.

Ava.

"I'm coming, sweetheart." He grabbed his jeans from the foot of the bed and slipped them on. He thought about retrieving his gun from the drawer of the bedside table, but he left it behind and ran to the door. He'd be scary enough charging into Ava's bedroom.

He pushed her door open and was instantly greeted by Maxie. The big dog glowed with the light from the moon seeping in around the curtains, the only illumination in the room. The dog seemed to be in distress, possibly because she wasn't able to wake her mistress. Ava was thrashing in the bed and crying out, in the full throes of a nightmare. He scrubbed his hand around Maxie's ears, soothing the beast. "I'm here. We'll help her. Don't you worry, girl."

Although he didn't want to alert anyone who might be watching the house, Luke didn't hesitate to turn on the lamp beside the bed. Ava's skin was flushed, her forehead dotted with perspiration. Her long hair clung to the dampness on her skin, masking her expression. But her moans were full of pain, and he couldn't stand by while she muttered pleas to be let go. Looking at the sheet and quilt twisted around her legs and the hair covering her face, he had a pretty good idea about where her mind was right now. He prayed that what he was about to do wouldn't make it worse.

He touched her.

"Ava." He grabbed the covers and pulled them from beneath her, unrolling her from her cloth prison. She screamed into her pillow. Luke pulled her hair away from her face and saw she was still in the grips of the scene that was haunting her. "I'm sorry, sweetheart." He grasped her by the shoulders and gave her a slight shake. "Ava, wake up." He tapped her cool cheek. "Ava!"

She came awake, knocking his hand from her face, screaming.

He retreated several inches away from her on the bed. Her eyes were wide, frightened, unfo-

cused in the moonlight. She blinked. They darkened as she looked at him. Luke nodded to the
furry caretaker sitting beside her, and Ava reached
for Maxie, burying her face in the dog's neck and
breathing deeply.

Luke watched for several minutes, making sure
she was all right. Gradually, she eased her grip on
the dog and Maxie licked Ava's face and neck,
earning a soft laugh and making Luke smile. Content that she could finish recovering without his
help, Luke pushed to his feet. "I'll leave the light
on for you, okay?"

Then she surprised him by reaching for his
hand. She lifted her beautiful eyes to his. "Thank
you."

When her grip tightened around his, he moved
a step closer. "Way to scare the team, Wallace."

She nodded. "Instead of trying to hash any of
this out, would you…?"

Luke sat on the edge of the bed again. He
switched hands and tucked a tendril of coffee-
colored hair behind her ear. "Anything. Just ask."

"Would you hold me? I'm so cold."

Whatever the woman needed. He didn't have
the power to say no. After folding the quilt and
sheet at the bottom of the bed so that nothing
could tangle between them or around her again,
Luke stretched out beside her, propping up the
pillows beneath his head and gathering her to his
side. She rested her head on his shoulder and her

hand in the middle of his chest where he threaded his fingers with hers and held them against the beat of his heart. Maxie curled up on the other side of her. Cocooned between their body heat, he doubted she needed any covers. "Better?"

She slipped her toes between his ankles, draping herself more fully against his side. "I'm such a mess."

He stroked his fingers through her hair with his free hand, lightly massaging her neck and back. "No, you're not. I'm afraid I've aggravated everything you're dealing with."

"But I'm *dealing* with it," she emphasized. "I might be online with my counselor every day this week as all these emotions surface again, but I'm not hiding from it anymore. Thank you for that."

"For giving you nightmares?"

She chuckled against his skin, and the brush of her lips felt like a kiss. "For waking me up. I don't mean tonight, although I appreciate that, too. Figuratively. You forced me to change the status quo. I realize I've been hiding away, not because of how others see me. But because of how I saw myself." Although their hands were still linked, she freed her index finger to trace gentle circles on his chest. Her touch left a trail of goose bumps in its wake and stoked a lambent desire deep inside him. "I thought of myself as a victim for two years, so that's how others treat me. But you don't."

"The people around here have known you

since you were a kid. They watched you grow up. They've seen the changes in you. People aren't always sure how to deal with it." Luke turned his head to press a kiss to her forehead. "I only know the woman who greeted me with a shotgun and then saved my life. She's pretty tough. Pretty resourceful. Doesn't give up. I know the woman in your books. She's talented. Speaks an important message about purpose and loyalty, never giving up hope, and fighting to do the right thing. I know the woman in my arms right now. She's beautiful. Tempting. Caring. I can't associate any of that with you being a victim."

"Absolutely the best compliments ever." This time, there was no mistaking the kiss she pressed beside the stitches on his shoulder. Then she rose up on her elbow beside him, her hair falling around him like a sable waterfall. "Thank you."

Luke raised his head to meet her halfway as she bent over to kiss him. Her lips were soft and pliant as they sampled each other with a leisurely thoroughness. Then her tongue swept across his lips and snuck inside to deepen the kiss. Luke was more than happy to oblige. He palmed the back of her head and took over. The other hand reached for her bottom and pulled her more fully on top of him. Her breasts pillowed against his chest and her hands roamed across his skin, stoking the fire she kindled inside him. There was no hiding how much he wanted her as her thigh slipped between his.

But when a cold nose butted his shoulder, then sniffed into Ava's hair, she laughed against his mouth and ended the kiss. Although parts of his body demanded they continue, the other, more important parts were thrilled that Ava settled back against his side with a heavy sigh.

"Better?" Ava nodded. "Do you want me to leave?"

She was still hugging him with her arms and body. "I want you to stay. Is that okay?"

"I'm very okay with that." Several minutes passed with them simply holding each other, and the fire inside him eased to a less urgent level. He caught her hand and stilled it when she started tracing those mindless circles across his chest again. "Do you need to talk about it?"

Her answer was a quick no. "Not my first nightmare. I'm guessing it won't be my last."

Luke was beginning to wonder if she'd let him hold her for a couple more hours of sleep, or if she'd ask him to leave so that she could completely relax. Until she said the words, however, he wasn't going anywhere. Holding Ava like this was a gift. Her touch felt as much a part of him as each and every memory he was slowly regaining. Her trust felt like he'd finally come home to the place where he belonged. But if all she needed from him was a few pushes out of her comfort zone and some tactile therapy, he wasn't going to ask for anything more.

Ignoring his body's demands for another kiss, Luke reached over Ava's back to stroke the dog, who had settled on the other side of her again. "Maxie's the real champion. She sounded the alarm."

"She's a natural. I got her to be a guard dog, but she's adapted these natural protective behaviors. She's the best thing ever to bring me out of an episode." Ava's fingers stopped their circles, and he felt her gaze snap up to the bottom of his chin. "Is that a turnoff? That I have a third party in bed with us?"

Luke was still petting Maxie. "You know I'm no stranger to PTSD. Dogs can be trained to do any number of things with repetitive practice and us understanding what a meaningful reward is to them. I'm guessing this one is all about the affection?"

Gradually, Ava relaxed again, as he accepted the Queen Mother of the Dragons on their team. "She won't turn her nose up at a treat, trust me. But yeah, she's a sucker for a belly rub or a scratch beneath her chin. Have you worked with dogs before?"

"Oh, yeah. Used them all the time with MP work. Can't beat a canine nose or ears when it comes to finding trouble or alerting to danger. Or comfort." Memories of a black-and-tan Belgian

Malinois ran through his mind. "My last K-9 partner was Axel. When I got promoted to a desk job, he was transferred to a new handler. But when it came time to retire him, I got him back as a pet for a couple of years. I miss that boy. Smartest dog I ever knew. Buried his ashes on the base where we served together after he passed."

"What base is that?"

"Fort Leonard Wood." They both stopped their petting at his automatic reply. Ava pushed herself to a sitting position and Luke met her knowing gaze. "I served at Fort Leonard Wood. That's where I ended my career. Earlier this year."

"That's in Missouri, right?"

"Yeah. It's an Army base. But different branches of the service and even civilians do police training there." Luke sat up beside her. The memories were flooding in now, all as clear as if they'd just happened. So much for relaxing and helping Ava fall back to sleep. He was breathing hard with excitement. Sitting still was no longer an option. He climbed out of bed and paced the room. "My buddy Joe Soldati works there. He took my place when I left. Are all my memories finally coming back?"

"Don't push it. Let's think about this one memory." Maxie woofed as Ava crawled to the edge of the bed and stood. "Is Soldati the friend you called before all this started?"

"I think so."

She picked up her cell phone from the bedside table and held it out to Luke. "Call him."

"It's four in the morning."

"Our time. It's 5 a.m. in Missouri, and you military guys like to rise early. Besides, if you called him three days ago with what you uncovered, and haven't checked in since then, he's worried about you. I would be."

He was a veteran Marine who had survived a car crash, dived off a cliff and taken a bullet. Why was he afraid to make this phone call?

Ava pushed the phone into his hand. "Call him. I'll be right here with you." She grinned. "In case you forget anything."

The tension in him broke and he laughed out loud as he took the phone. "Wiseacre."

Since he couldn't recall a phone number, he called the information operator instead. "I need a number for Fort Leonard Wood Army base near Waynesville, Missouri." After she dialed a general office on the base for him, Luke identified himself. "Captain Luke Broughton, USMC, Retired." He rattled off his serial number as if he was still active duty. "Captain Joe Soldati, military police. I know it's early, but does he happen to be on base?"

The corporal manning the communication center wrote down Ava's phone number and took Luke's message. Thirty minutes later, a plan was in place and the backup Luke needed was on its way to Wyoming. Joe had given him plenty of grief about waking him from a good night's sleep, but not as much grief as he'd given Luke for missing the flight he'd promised to be on Saturday morning. Apparently, Luke had given his friend an abridged version of what he'd uncovered, and arranged a rendezvous to turn over the evidence he had on BDS.

"When you didn't get off that plane, I thought the worst," Joe confessed. "If what you say is true, you're damn lucky to be alive."

Luke looked across the room to Ava, who was settling Maxie into her bed with a rawhide chew and eavesdropping on every word. "I couldn't have done it on my own. You'll take care of things from your end?"

"I've got all the phone calls made. All I need is my star witness to come out of hiding and debrief my superiors and the JAG office."

"I'll owe you one, buddy."

"Damn straight you will." Joe Soldati had served under Luke for several years before getting the promotion. He knew the guy was a lot of guff and wiseassery, but as solid and dependable as they came. "This is at least a three-beer and an introduce-me-to-your-sister favor, Broughton."

"I don't have a sister."

"Then I'll settle for the beer."

"You're on."

Then Joe got back to business. "My go bag is packed. I'll contact the JAG office while I'm in the air to see if they want to get the feds involved at this point. My contacts at the Wyoming state police have been waiting for a follow-up call from me. I'll get on the horn with them. The cavalry's coming. Keep your head down until we get there."

"Roger that." Ava crawled back into the bed and patted the mattress beside her, telling him he was welcome to rejoin her when the conversation ended. Every cell in Luke's body leaped at the invitation. "And Joe? You know those *Bonecrusher Chronicles* books you got me into?"

"Yeah?"

"The woman I told you about who's been helping me?" Ava's momentary frown was probably her worrying that he was going to give away her secret identity. She had to know him better than that by now. "She reminds me of Willow Storm."

Joe laughed. "Lucky dog. See you in a few hours."

After disconnecting the call, Luke set the phone beside her laptop and crawled onto the bed to sit beside her. Although he knew they wouldn't be completely safe until Joe and his team arrived, criminals were identified and arrests were made, Luke felt his guard dropping, knowing the authorities were on their way to give him and Ava true sanctuary. He felt like they'd done this a hundred times when he draped his arm around her shoulders and she snuggled against his side; it felt so natural.

He pressed a kiss to her temple. "Once again, you've helped me find the truth. Ever think about a career in law enforcement? You'd make a hell of an interrogator."

"I've already got a pretty good gig."

"Writing books?"

"Being with you." Her fingers were doing that lazy circle thing on his skin again. This time farther down the flat of his stomach, sending tiny electric pulses straight down to his groin. "Do male readers really think Willow is hot?"

"Oh, yeah." His voice came out as a throaty growl.

Her fingers stopped their magic spell and she sat up on her knees to face him. "Luke, I want to try... I want...you."

"Ava, I don't deserve—"

"Don't you go all noble on me now. Larkin Bonecrusher is a rogue. And I know... I mean, earlier at the cave, and a while ago when we kissed... I could feel... I think you want me, too."

He glanced down at the tightness pushing against his zipper. "I'm not hiding the fact I do." He cupped her face between his hands, reading the certainty in her eyes. "Are you sure? You don't owe me anything."

"No." She smiled. "You owe me."

Well, hell's bells. He could add seductress to the list of things this woman did well. "Luke Broughton reporting for duty."

He pulled her into his lap and covered her mouth with his. When he pushed his tongue between her lips, she opened for him, welcoming his claim. While he feasted on her mouth, her hands mimicked his, framing his face, sliding into his hair, learning all the places that liked to be touched. She tore her lips from his, clamping her teeth gently on the point of his chin, eliciting a feral growl.

"Whatever you want, Ava," he promised. "However you want it." He blazed his own trail down the side of her neck, paying special attention to the bundle of nerves at the base of her throat that made her squirm each time he teased it with his beard or soothed it with his tongue.

"I can't guarantee how good—"

"Don't go there." He lifted his head to press a hard kiss to her swollen lips before pulling back and settling his hands at the relatively neutral position at her waist. "We're in this together, remember? If there's anything you don't like—if you need to stop, I will. Scaring you in any way would be worse than not being with you."

Although he was breathing hard from the things this woman did to him, Luke held himself as still as humanly possible.

But his warrior princess was having none of that. She grasped his wrists and pulled his hands around to cup her bottom. "But I'm brave." She leaned in and kissed him.

"You are." He squeezed her bottom, holding her close as she came in for another kiss.

"I'm tough." Their lips got intimately acquainted while she unsnapped his jeans and slowly pulled down the zipper.

Luke groaned into her mouth. "The toughest."

"I'm tempting." Her eyes locked onto his as she slid her hand inside his pants.

He hissed at the way his body jumped to her touch. "Yes."

Luke couldn't hold back anymore. If she asked him to stop or give her space, he would. But until she gave any hint of panic setting in, he was going after what he wanted so desperately. He tugged the T-shirt over Ava's head and snapped her to him, needing the feel of skin to skin. He claimed her mouth with a deep, drugging kiss, hinting at his intent, assuring her of his desire. He licked and nipped and kissed his way down to that bundle of nerves and lower still until he sucked the pebbled tip of one pretty breast into his mouth.

One moment she was arching into him with a breathy moan, the next she was sitting back, covering herself with her hands. "Should we turn the light off?"

Luke eased himself up to a sitting position beside her. This was the hesitation he'd been worried about, the changing of her mind that he would respect. "I thought you'd be more comfortable with it on."

"But you'll see all my scars."

Luke bit down on his cry of relief. This wasn't about stopping. This was about reassurance, and the healing they seemed to give each other. "I'll show you mine if you show me yours."

Ava's mouth opened in a startled O, then quickly closed. "It's not a competition."

"Wanna bet?" He gingerly shucked off his jeans and tossed them to the floor. He pointed to the wound on his shoulder. "Bullet hole, obviously." Then he tapped the stitches on his knee. "Split this open on a rock." He pulled down the waistband of his shorts and brushed his fingers over his hip. "Bomb fragments. Hip surgery."

She was laughing by the time he got to the three dots on the back of his hand he'd gotten holding a sparkler one Fourth of July as a boy. "Enough. You're a stunning man. I watched you yesterday morning while you were sleeping." Her cheeks turned rosy with an embarrassed blush. "I guess I'm a bit of a voyeur."

"So, you can treat me like a piece of meat, but I can't enjoy ogling you?" Luke traced his finger along the mark on her chest. He leaned in and brushed the gentlest of kisses against her injured cheek. "I know the scars are here. I know everything they symbolize. But I don't see them when I look at you. I see *you*."

"You're sure?"

"Sweetheart, I'm a man. At the moment, I only

mouth in a kiss. He slipped his thumb in between them where they were linked and pressed the sensitive bud that took her to the top of the mountain. And as Ava gasped his name—*his* name, "Luke..."—beside his ear, the tension in him released. He thrust into her one more time, topping the crest and following her down the other side.

Chapter Thirteen

Ava slept soundly, free from nightmares, claimed by the most beautiful kind of exhaustion. After waking with the sunrise to put Maxie out for her morning constitutional and feed her beloved pet, she went back upstairs to return to Luke's arms and discover other sorts of pleasure that didn't require the protection they lacked.

She'd learned that the numbers beneath the tattoo were a tribute to the men and women he'd lost in his unit, marking the date of their ultimate sacrifice. Ava had kissed each number, then kissed the man bearing the tribute, before he'd pulled the quilt over them both and she'd drifted off with her lips smiling against the eagle, globe and anchor.

The morning sun was shining brightly through the gaps around the window when she awoke to the suffocating sensation of being pressed down onto the bed. She came awake, gasping for air, shoving at the weight that pinned her down.

"It's okay, Ava. It's me."

Even as Luke moved the arm and leg that he'd thrown over her while they slept, she was rolling off the edge of the bed. She tumbled onto her knees, then quickly stood up, orienting herself to her surroundings and the sound of Luke's voice. By the time she focused in on him standing on the opposite side of the bed in his boxer-briefs, she knew she'd ruined the beautiful night they'd shared.

"I'm sorry," she apologized. "For a minute, I forgot you were with me. If I had opened my eyes first—"

"Stop it," he ordered, his slitted eyes raking over her from head to toe. Ava hugged her arms around herself, knowing that she'd hurt him, but not knowing the words to say to make it right. But then Luke was striding around the bed, pulling her into his arms and giving her the kind of hug she really needed. "I'm not angry at you. I'm mad because you think you need to apologize. Neither one of us is going to be fixed overnight. There are going to be setbacks, but as long as we're working through them together, I can handle it. I'm in this for the long haul with you, sweetheart. I just need to know that you're in the fight with me."

Sighing with relief, Ava snaked her arms around his waist. What she and Luke had shared this weekend had been more than therapeutic. He hadn't just reawakened her courage. He'd awakened her heart. Her feelings for this man were new and tender and strong, and she didn't want to jeopardize this precious gift before she had the chance to explore where a relationship between them might lead once they got past the obstacles of her PTSD, his amnesia and people who wanted him dead.

How could she not love a man who wasn't scared of her mood swings, and who kissed like a man on a mission. Wait. Love? Was that where her thoughts had gone? Was that what her heart wanted?

Clearly needing to start this morning over again, Ava opted for humor. "'I just need to know that you're in the fight with me.' That's good. Can I use that line in the book?"

He laughed. "As long as you understand that my promise to you is real, not fiction."

Luke stiffened a split second before she heard the crunch of gravel in the distance and Maxie woofed a warning downstairs as a vehicle approached the cabin.

Luke didn't bother to ask if she was expecting visitors. "This conversation isn't over." He released her to pull on his jeans and dashed across the hallway to grab a T-shirt, boots and his gun.

Ava pulled underwear and a tank top from her dresser. "You need to get to Stormhaven. Now. Take the back door straight out to the trees. You'll run into the creek. Turn north and follow it about fifteen, twenty minutes to the cave, depending on how fast you move. They'll never see you."

He reappeared in the doorway, tucking his gun into the back of his jeans. "You're coming with me."

"No. I can distract them while you get away. Nobody's after me. I need you to be safe. Until your friend gets here, we're still on our own." She gestured to the rumpled bed. "I want to do this again. I want to do it better."

He took two steps, palmed the back of her neck and pulled her onto her toes for a hard, quick kiss. "Sweetheart, it doesn't get any better than last night." Her cheeks were on fire at that blunt reassurance. "But I'm more than willing to practice if that's what you want." She laughed and they traded another quick kiss. "Now wipe that blush off your face and throw some pants on so you can answer the door."

Ava pulled on her socks and jeans while Luke peeked out the window to see the approaching vehicles. "Looks like the sheriff's car and a black SUV." He let the curtain fall shut again. "I don't like this." He picked up her cell phone and tucked it into the back pocket of her jeans while she zipped the front. "You're coming with me."

"No." She grabbed her boots and pushed him into the hallway, hurrying him down the stairs in front of her. "Brandon won't hurt me. He's still trying to get me to go out with him again. You, on the other hand, he'll probably slap in jail."

"Ava—"

"Luke. You're not supposed to be here. Don't be here." She picked up the backpack of supplies they'd prepped the night before, in case they'd needed to make an escape like this, and handed it to him. "If whoever is in that black SUV is the man who tried to kill you, what's to stop him if he finds you here. And what's to stop him from killing Brandon and me, too, so there are no witnesses."

"Damn, I hate that you're right."

She laid her hand against his jaw, stroking her fingers through his beard. "Sometimes, the only way to win a battle is to avoid it until you're ready to fight."

"Larkin Bonecrusher, Book Two."

"You do read my books."

"You've got my new cell number?" Ava nodded. "Call as soon as you can and let me know what's going on. If I don't see your face in an hour, I will come back for you."

"It might not be safe."

"If anything happens to you, none of this matters."

"Hang on." She ran back to the living room and retrieved a key from her desk. She looped the lanyard attached to it around his neck. "The key to the closet where my gun safe is. The combination is JMW-7334. In case you and your Marine buddies need some backup and I'm not here."

"JMW-7334," he repeated back to her. "I will come back for you." He brushed his fingers into her hair and tucked it behind her ear before turning to the dog, who watched them curiously. "You. Keep her safe."

The crunch of gravel stopped, and they both knew their unwanted guests had pulled into the driveway.

"Go." Ava closed the door behind Luke and watched him run to the tree line and disappear.

Maxie barked and got up as the first car door closed out front. Ava took the time to tie her boots and button her blouse before answering the repeated knocking at her front door.

She plaited her hair into a loose braid and pulled it over her shoulder to mask her damaged cheek before unlocking the door and opening it to greet Sheriff Stout. Brandon wore mirrored sunglasses beneath the bill of his hat, making it impossible to read his expression. All she could see was her own pale reflection. She needed to do better than cringe and chase people away if she was going to help Luke.

You're smart. You've got skills now. You're a survivor. You've got this, Ava.

"Hi." Brandon pushed her inside and closed the door before she could see who was in the second vehicle. "What are you doing here?"

"A guy can't come see his best girl?"

"With company?" She moved around him to

peek through the sidelight and realized the SUV's windows were tinted. She couldn't see the driver or if anyone was with him. "Can I get you some coffee or iced tea? Do your friends want anything?"

When had Ava Wallace ever invited anyone inside her remote home for tea and cookies? But Brandon didn't seem to notice her unusual politeness. Maybe she was finally acting the way he expected her to.

"Nah." He took off his hat and worked the brim between his hands. "Sorry to bug you. I guess you were working?"

Not exactly. But out loud, she answered, "Yes."

"Well, this won't take too long." Was the man in the other vehicle not coming in? Or worse, was he walking around her property, searching for Luke? "I understand you talked to a man named Hauser in town yesterday. I'm helping him look for an employee of his who's gone missing."

"Missing?" It was too easy to play dumb with a man who expected her to be clueless about the dangers of the world. Maxie leaned into Ava's thigh and she gladly ran her fingers over the dog's head. She needed to stay calm to keep up this friendly facade. "That sounds terrible. His family must be so worried about him."

"According to Hauser, he doesn't have a family. No wife or kids. Dead parents. Only child."

She wondered if Luke had remembered that.

That was probably one reason why he'd formed such tight bonds with his fellow Marines. They were his family. It was also probably why he'd taken the deaths of Ryan Voltaggio and the rest of his unit so hard. "Well, I'm sure someone's missing him."

"The people he works for would sure like to find him. Hauser wants to come in and ask you some questions. See if you've remembered anything helpful about the man you brought in. Doc Russell is looking for him, too. He's worried your John Doe could be a danger to himself. With that head injury, if he passes out and can't get help, he could die." Brandon took off his sunglasses and tucked them into his shirt pocket, finally letting her see the concern lining his eyes. "And since he took off before I got a chance to interview him, I wanted to know if he'd contacted you. Maybe to thank you."

Maxie circled around Ava's legs, perhaps sensing something that Ava couldn't. Had she missed the other man getting out of his SUV? "Like I told Mr. Hauser yesterday, I couldn't tell if the picture he showed me matches the man I met or not. I haven't seen him since."

When the dog trotted to the front door and woofed, Brandon rolled his eyes with an impatient huff. "Would you mind putting Maxie in her crate?"

"Yeah, as a matter of fact, I—"

"Hauser's waiting outside, and you know how Maxie is with strangers. The sooner we can have this conversation, the sooner we can get out of your hair."

The sharpness of his tone was a little unexpected. "Couldn't I talk to him out on the front porch? You know I don't like company at the house."

Brandon caught her hand and squeezed it. "Please, Ave. I need your help." Maybe Hauser had already threatened Brandon. *Get the weird recluse to talk or your brakes might go out, too.*

If she'd really been playing her part, she would have pulled free of his grasp. But his plea was her Achilles' heel. The last time she'd stopped to help a man…had been Luke Broughton. And her time with him had changed her life. He'd changed her self-perception and he'd changed her heart. The least she could do was help a friend she'd known since she was eight years old.

"Okay. I'll talk to him. For you."

"Thanks, babe." It wasn't an act when Brandon hugged her. Her pulse pounded in her ears and her breath locked in her chest. She couldn't stop herself from pushing away.

"The Rule of Three, Brandon. Let go." As soon as he released her, she whistled for Maxie and led her to her crate in the kitchen. She paused for a few seconds to pet the dog, centering herself.

"Sorry, girl. Not everybody knows what a love bug you are."

She'd just clicked the latch shut when Maxie let out a warning bark.

In the next second, a scarf looped over her head, settling in front of her eyes and pulling her back. Ava screamed and scratched at the silky material as a knot tightened at the back of her head, catching strands of hair and pinching her scalp.

She scratched at the hands that were tying the blindfold on. The same hands cinched her arms and lifted her off her feet. "Stop! Why are you doing this?" Something else looped around her eyes, tighter, elasticized, blocking out even the light. Ava twisted, breaking one hand free, and clawed at the nightmare against her skin. "You don't understand. Please don't do this! Brandon!"

The arms that carried her tightened their grip. "It's for your own safety, babe. If you don't see faces, you can't identify anyone, and there's no reason to hurt you. I asked them if we could handle it this way."

"Them?"

"I don't want you to get hurt. I love you. I want a future with you."

Ava was screaming, thrashing against the restraint of his arms and chest. She kicked at his shins, tried to throw him off balance. She was sinking into the darkness, helpless again. "Do you

know what a panic attack is? Did you ever wonder why I have them?"

"This is the only way. These people don't like
witnesses."

Think, Ava! Stay in the moment. With Luke
fleeing for his life and Maxie caged, no one could
help her if she got trapped in the past. She had to
be strong. She had to be smart.

There was a flaw in Brandon's logic. She might
not know who he was talking about, but she knew
him. And if he was involved with Bell Design Systems, then she was a witness to that involvement.
She wasn't safe. Brandon might not even realize
that he wasn't safe.

The front door opened. She felt the warmth of
the sun on her skin, but she couldn't see anything.
"Brandon, please!"

"It's all right." Brandon was shouting past her to
someone else. "The dog is secured, and she can't
see anything."

"Let go of me!"

She heard footsteps on the wood porch. More
than one set of footsteps. At least one person was
heavy enough to make the steps creak.

"Why is she flailing around like that?" an unfamiliar voice asked. "Tie her up. If she raises her
voice again, put a gag in her mouth."

She felt light-headed when the first metal brace-
let locked around her wrist. She took a wild swing
at her captor, but Brandon caught her arm and

pulled it behind her with a painful wrench to her shoulder. "Come on, Ave. I'm trying to save you here. Cooperate."

With the handcuffs locked around her wrists, Brandon dragged her back into the living room and pushed her down onto the sofa. As he warned her to stay put, she heard the other men moving through her house. Opening doors, clinking dishes in the kitchen. Rifling through her desk.

"What are they doing? Please take off the blindfold. I have a phobia—"

"There are no BDS flash drives here." That voice she knew, didn't she? But it was hard to place it with the terror swirling around inside her head.

"Brandon, I can't see."

"That's the whole idea. Come on, baby. Stop acting crazy. These men need to ask you a few questions."

"And I have to be blindfolded and handcuffed to answer?" And poor Maxie, growling and barking, desperate to get to her. Someone banged on her cage and she stopped for a second, then barked again, sounding a lot less like a big, friendly galoot and a lot more like a beast who wanted to take someone's head off. "You're a fool, Brandon. No wonder I couldn't confide in you."

"Confide in me about what?"

"Didn't you ever wonder why I'd changed when I moved back here?" She rocked back and forth, willing the past to stay in the past, knowing she needed to focus on the present to survive.

"It's okay, Ave. I'm taking care of everything."

"I don't need to be taken care of."

"Do you know who I am, Ms. Baines?" A new voice spoke. An older voice. One she didn't recognize.

Brandon squeezed her shoulder and she nearly jumped off the couch. "I told you this is Ava Wallace."

"He doesn't know?"

Ava forced herself to stop rocking and shrugged. "I don't know what you're talking about."

"Don't be stupid. I dislike stupid people." Then this man must despise Brandon.

She heard footsteps on the stairs. One man. She wondered how many were still here with her.

The older man's voice continued. "I know you're A. L. Baines, Miss Wallace. My daughters are huge fans of yours. They have a crush on some knight named Larkin Bonecrusher."

Play dumb. "*The Bonecrusher Chronicles*. I've read those, too. Pretty entertaining books."

"I also know what happened to you in Chicago two years ago." Everything in Ava went still. "I know that Detective Gabriel Charles has made an arrest based on a recent murder, and he will be calling you later today about identifying the man and giving a sworn deposition."

"You hacked into my case file at CPD?"

"I'm pretty good with technology. What I don't know personally, I can hire people from all over the world to do for me." This man thought he had the upper hand. Right now, he probably did. But this fight wasn't over. She needed to assess her enemy and gather evidence until the moment came to fight this battle. "I needed to know who I was working with and the best way to get what I wanted from you."

"Which is?"

"I believe you know more about Luke Broughton than you let on to Sheriff Stout."

"And you thought inciting a panic attack by sending me a message from my kidnapper would ensure my cooperation?"

"I figured—correctly—that reminding you of that trauma would throw you off whatever game you've been playing with my men." The man sank onto the cushion beside her, and she instinctively shifted away from the invisible threat. "You see, I'm very good at reading people, Ms. Baines—"

"It's Wallace."

"—and I believe you've been lying."

No more pretense. No more playing dumb. "Is there something I could help you with, Mr. Bell? It is Mr. Bell, isn't it?"

Brandon swore beside her. "Damn it, Ave. I can't protect you if you know too much."

"Don't you need a warrant to search my house?" she challenged.

Brandon might be on edge, but Gregory Bell wasn't fazed. "I'm looking for Luke Broughton."

"I don't know anyone by that name."

"Perhaps not. You took him to the hospital with amnesia, but he escaped. Vanished from existence, it would seem. Now, whatever name he might be using, I think you do know him."

"Intimately, from the look of things." The man who'd gone upstairs returned. "There are men's toiletries in the bathroom. The bed in her room has seen some action."

"You slept with him?" Brandon raged above her. "You won't give me the time of day, and you slept with that stranger?"

"Better him than you."

She never saw the hand that slapped her across the face. Tears soaked into the cloth covering her eyes and burned along her cheek as she cowered in the corner of the sofa. But it wasn't pain that finally made her cry. It was the memories. Her skin crawled with the imprint of knives cutting into her. She anticipated the next touch, the next cut, never knowing if she would bleed or gag at the mockery of tenderness. Her fingers ached to latch on to Maxie's familiar warmth. Her heart needed Luke to remind her that she could handle this. She could handle anything.

She turned her head toward Brandon's heavy steps pacing beside her. "How long have you been part of this?"

"On and off over the years," he answered. "They paid me a lot of money to look the other way when they conducted certain business up at the Ridgerunner. I got rid of your boyfriend's car for them."

"You started that fire? What if it had spread to Mr. Harold's trailer?"

"What if you stop talking." Gregory Bell didn't care about a dishonored badge or a friendship betrayed. "Where is Broughton?"

Ava understood that the weakest link here was Brandon. "I know him better after seventy-two hours than I know you after twenty-seven years. You're working with these people?"

"I'm looking for a fugitive. He's a danger to you, Ave. Can't you see that?"

"You're the danger because you won't stand up and do the right thing. They're a danger to our military. To our country."

Metal screeched against the kitchen's tile floor as Maxie threw her weight against the side of her crate.

"Damn it, Maxie, shut up!"

When she heard the snap of Brandon's holster, Ava lurched to her feet and charged at him. "Don't you dare!"

Another pair of hands clamped down on her arms and pulled her against a solid chest. She screamed at the startling touch. There was another grab and she screamed again.

"Quiet," Brandon warned, his grip cutting off the circulation above her elbow. "You keep your hands off her," he warned the other man. Although she hadn't heard his voice enough to be certain it was Roy Hauser, the bulk of his build and the slab of protective armor she'd slammed into made her doubt it could be anybody else. Brandon stroked her hair, no doubt trying to placate her, but simply reminding her of the blindfold knotted at the back of her head. "I'm sorry I hit you, baby. Cooperate with me now, and I'll protect you. Can we get her out of here now?"

"I'm not the only one who's changed, Brandon." As much as she had once treasured their friendship, any loyalty she'd felt to this man was done.

"Patience, Sheriff," Gregory Bell spoke again. "We can assume Captain Broughton is hiding nearby. A gunshot will bring him running. We'd be at the disadvantage. He has to bring me the flash drive. And I need to know anyone he's shared that information with over the last seventy-two hours before we kill him. With your temper, I'm afraid you'll shoot him before I get everything I need from him."

The door opened and Brandon dragged her outside. "You said you wouldn't hurt Ava. That she would still be mine."

"Yours?" But no one was listening to her.

Maxie was barking to raise the dead. The men had to shout to be heard.

"What are you going to do with her?" Brandon asked.

"Take her with us, of course. Put her in my car. I have a feeling she'll make fine bait."

A vehicle door opened, and she was shoved into a back seat. "Brandon, don't do this," she pleaded. "I won't come back from this trip. Neither of us will."

She heard a blam from somewhere in the distance and a hard thump on the ground at her feet.

She didn't need to see to recognize that sound. That was a blast from a Browning double-barrel shotgun. Brandon Stout was dead.

Chapter Fourteen

"What the hell is going on here?" Gregory Bell shouted. "Who fired those shots?"

She heard another vehicle door opening, feet scrabbling through the gravel.

"Ava! Stay down!" *Luke.*

Her heart surged in her chest. Luke was here.

That brave, wonderful man hadn't gone to Stormhaven to save himself. He'd doubled back to the cabin to save her. He'd raided her gun safe and was going to battle against the men whom she was sure intended to kill her once she'd served her purpose.

"Side of the garage, boss."

Ava heard an exchange of gunfire. Smaller caliber weaponry this time. Handguns.

She huddled down in the seat.

"Call off your goon, Bell!" Luke shouted once the bullets stopped flying. "I've got what you came for. I'm putting down my gun and coming out. Let Ava go."

Ava stiffened. This wasn't the plan. This was so not the plan. What happened to Option B?

"Luke! Don't do it!" she yelled. "They'll kill you!"

"Hands where I can see them, Captain." Roy Hauser gave the order she prayed Luke wouldn't obey. "Show me the flash drive."

Luke chuckled. "Do you want me to reach into my pocket or hold my hands up?"

Gregory Bell wasn't waiting to see who won this duel of wills. "On the ground, Broughton. Hands on your head. Roy, you search his pockets."

"He has a gun hidden on him, sir. I know how he thinks."

"I gave you an order."

Hauser capitulated to his CEO's command. "On the ground, Captain. And don't try anything funny."

"What? Like pretend to be my friend? Act all concerned when I bring you evidence that someone inside BDS is selling company technology to Chinese insurgents? That kind of funny?"

"He's baiting you, Roy. Search him!"

Then he heard Hauser curse. Something heavy hit the ground and there was a scuffle. The horrid thud of fist hitting bone. A moan of pain.

"Luke!"

Gravel flying. A breathless curse.

Then the fighting stopped. Ava held her breath until she heard Luke's stern voice. "Don't do it, Roy. Things look a little different when you're staring down the barrel end of a gun, don't they?"

"You and what army are going to take us down?" Hauser taunted.

Something small hit the rocks. "Put those on," Luke ordered. "Chain yourself to the bumper. By order of the United States Marine Corps, I'm placing you under arrest for attempted murder and a whole bunch of other treasonous crimes that my buddies at JAG and the state police are putting together right now."

Hauser muttered a curse, but judging by the clank of metal on metal, he was securing himself to the bumper of one of the SUVs. "I was carrying out orders. You understand that. You weren't the first problem I was told to eliminate, and you won't be the last. It wasn't anything personal."

"Funny how getting run off the road, shot and being forced to dive over the edge of a cliff feel personal."

She heard someone breathing erratically and feared that Luke had taken a blow to the head or reopened the wound on his shoulder.

"Luke? Are you all right?"

But Luke Broughton was a Marine on a mission. "You're next, Bell. You've got nobody left to do your dirty work for you. It's you and me."

"Stop all this pointless prattle." Bell's voice was right beside Ava. She curled up her legs and pushed across the seat. How had she missed his approach? She jumped at the hand that clamped around her ankle and dragged her from the SUV.

The moment her feet hit the ground, she stumbled over Brandon's inert body. But an arm locked around her neck and shoulder and pulled her upright. She felt Gregory Bell's hot breath against her ear and the cold steel of a gun press into her temple. "I still have the upper hand, Broughton. Hand over the flash drive. Now!"

Luke cursed. For the first time in this whole showdown, he sounded like he was losing it. "You put a blindfold on her? You're lucky I don't shoot you like I did Stout. You want this flash drive? You let her go first."

She felt Bell shake his head as the tip of the gun ground against her skull. "The flash drive first. Then your girlfriend and I are driving out of here. I'll drop her off at one of the scenic overlooks and you can pick her up there."

"And trust that you're not going to push her off the side of the mountain so she can't testify against you, either? You hired me to be smarter than that."

"Fine. You've got no shot, Marine. Keep your evidence against me. I'm keeping her."

"No! I'm not your victim!" Ava stomped on Bell's foot, and threw her hips back against him.

"Don't struggle, Ava."

"I'm not going with him. If he doesn't care whether you live or die, he certainly doesn't care about me."

"Summon the dragon, Ava."

She froze at the odd request. "What?"

"Summon the dragon."

And then she understood. *Sometimes, the only way to win a battle is to avoid it until you're ready to fight.*

Larkin and Willow were ready to fight.

Ava pulled her teeth to her lips and gave a shrill whistle. "Maxie! Come!"

"What the…?"

Gregory Bell must have seen the pony-size dog charging toward him a second too late. Maxie leaped and her great, muscular paws hit Bell, knocking the gun from his hand, loosing his grip on Ava and sending all three of them tumbling to the ground.

Luke was there before Ava got to her feet. "It's me, sweetheart," he announced a split second before he unknotted the blindfold and whisked it off. "I'm so sorry they did that to you."

She blinked against the overly bright sunshine. "I'm okay. I kept it together." It took a moment to bring Luke into focus. Oh, no. He *was* bleeding. A spot of red stained the front of his T-shirt. "You're hurt. Your wound opened up."

"The stitches split when Hauser punched me there. I'll live." She could also see that his stance was strong and unwavering, just like the Hellcat he had trained on Gregory Bell. The CEO looked a lot less powerful lying in his dusty suit on the ground with an unhappy guard dog standing over him. "Where is the key to the cuffs?" he asked.

"On Brandon."

Keeping his gun trained on his former boss, Luke knelt beside Brandon's still body and checked his pockets until he found the key to unlock Ava. Then he handed her the cuffs. "Put them on him."

Ava handcuffed Gregory Bell's wrists behind his back and came back to stand at Luke's side. She brought Maxie with her, smoothing her fingers on the dog's head and praising her as she leaned against Ava's thigh.

"I'm a good man, Mr. Bell." Luke kept glancing down the road, as if he expected to see more company on her doorstep. "I did the right thing. And you tried to kill me and the woman I love for it. This time, the good guys win."

The woman he loved? Ava glanced up at Luke's rugged profile. Earlier, when he'd said he loved her, she thought he'd been caught up in the heat of the moment, riding the emotional catharsis of their lovemaking. But now he was telling the bad guy that he loved her? Oh, man, did they have a lot to talk about. And she needed to get back to her computer. She'd conquered the love scene. She'd just figured out that Larkin and Willow would exchange those three little words on the battlefield.

"Uh-oh. I know that look." Luke reached over to capture her hand in his, startling her from her thoughts. "Sorry."

Ava squeezed his hand and held on tight when

he would have pulled away. "Before anything else happens, I love you, too."

Luke leaned in and claimed her lips in a hard kiss that spoke volumes about all that had passed between them, and all that might yet come to pass. By the time he pulled away, there was a trio of state police cars racing up the gravel road.

A cloud of dust settled over them as the cars pulled to a sudden stop and several armed men and women streamed out, splitting up and going to each of the three men Luke and Maxie had taken down. A stocky, black-haired man in a tan uniform emblazoned with several ribbons and captain's bars headed straight to them.

Luke returned his weapon to his ankle holster and reached out to shake the Marine's hand. "Joe Soldati. I never thought I'd be this happy to see your ugly face." Joe pulled Luke in for a back-slapping hug that made him wince before pulling away. "This is Ava Wallace."

"Ma'am." Joe touched the brim of his cap in a polite greeting before turning his attention back to Luke. "You do understand the concept of civilian life, don't you, Cap? You're supposed to take it easy. Not risk life and limb for your country anymore."

"Old habits die hard, I guess."

"Leave it to you, Cap. Having all the fun without us. I would have been here sooner except we took a wrong turn at some Podunk town about twenty miles down the road."

Ava and Luke answered the uniformed MP at the same time. "Pole Axe."

"When you said you wanted a change of scenery, I had no idea. You okay, ma'am?"

Luke slipped his arm around her waist, pulling her to his side. "I've got her, Joe."

"Would you at least let me arrest some of these people?"

"Gladly."

Several hours later, the sun was a red-orange fireball sinking behind the western ridge of the mountains when Ava and Maxie strolled onto the porch to join Luke where he'd stretched out in a rocking chair to reread her first book. He slipped a bookmark between the pages and set the book on the bench beside him. "Did you get your chapter written?"

Ava nodded. She was glad to see he'd changed into a clean shirt after another trip to the clinic to get his stitches resewn, fill out the forms with his proper name and take care of his bill. "Did Joe get all the bad guys off my property?"

"Uh-huh." Luke spread his knees apart and invited her to take a seat on his lap. "Joe's got a ton of paperwork that will keep him in Cheyenne for a few days. When he's done with that, he'd like to come back and spend some time here. Get to know you. See if I'm good enough for you."

"A true friend of yours would always be welcome here. Did I hear you say he was the one who got you interested in *The Bonecrusher Chronicles*?"

Luke nodded. "I'm afraid if he finds out you're A. L. Baines, we'll never get rid of him."

"We? Are you staying?"

"I'd like to. You said I could stay until I got the flash drive or regained my memory. I handed the flash drive over to Joe so, technically, I don't have it. And… I can't seem to remember where I put my car keys."

"They're in your pocket. Neither excuse holds water." She stroked her fingers across his lips and watched his eyes narrow to silvery-green slits as she ran her palms across all the interesting textures of his face. "Is there any other reason you want to stay? I'm grateful for everything you've done for me, but now that your quest has ended, what's to keep you here?"

His hands settled at her waist and he pulled her closer, tucking the crown of her hair beneath his chin. "I'm the one who's grateful. You saved my life. You love me. I'm finally getting to read a new Bonecrusher novel." She swatted him on the arm for that last one and he laughed. "You and I make an even better team than Larkin and Willow, and I'd like to stay. Besides, our quest to get all the bad guys isn't over yet. I intend to go with you to Chicago to confront your attacker and help the police nail that guy."

"You'd do that for me?"

"I'll move to Chicago to be with you if that's what you want once everything is settled."

Ava tilted her face to his. "What if I want to stay in Wyoming?"

He lowered his lips to hers. "Well, Pole Axe is going to need a new sheriff."

* * * * *

Look for a brand-new series from USA TODAY bestselling author Julie Miller coming later in 2021!

Get 4 FREE REWARDS!

We'll send you 2 FREE Books plus 2 FREE Mystery Gifts.

Harlequin Presents books feature the glamorous lives of royals and billionaires in a world of exotic locations, where passion knows no bounds.

FREE Value Over $20